## MEET THE PATIENT

Wires ran from her tangled raven-black hair. They were attached to a console with a single flashing red light. The console was cheap, crude, the kind you could find in sleazy 'dromes and bars all over the City, the kind that damaged as many brain functions as it enhanced.

Karmade cursed. He stepped close to her, heart pounding. *Quasar Zant*— He peeled up her eyelid. There was nothing but white; her iris was rolled all the way up into her head.

Agitated, he looked at the transducer readouts.

The level and scope of stimulation was incredible; almost every part of her brain was entrained in a jagged wave form he had never seen before, at 75 millivolts. The stimulation chronograph stood at 20.33 hours.

Maximum safe stimulation time for hypothalamic transducers was about four hours.

Panic blared in him. He gave Quasar Zant a quick examination with sweat-slick hands. Her skin was cold, grayish, her pulse and breathing barely detectable. She might already be dead, he realized, the pounding rhythms of the transducer keeping up a counterfeit of life as they rammed through her brain—

# QUASAR

## JAMIL NASIR

BANTAM BOOKS
NEW YORK TORONTO
LONDON SYDNEY AUCKLAND

QUASAR

*A Bantam Spectra Book / November 1995*

SPECTRA *and the portrayal of a boxed "s" are trademarks of Bantam Books, a
division of Bantam Doubleday Dell Publishing Group, Inc.*

ISBN 0-553-56886-8

*Published simultaneously in the United States and Canada*

*Bantam Books are published by Bantam Books, a division of Bantam Double-
day Dell Publishing Group, Inc. Its trademark, consisting of the words "Bantam Books" and the portrayal of a rooster, is Registered in U.S. Patent and
Trademark Office and in other countries. Marca Registrada. Bantam Books,
1540 Broadway, New York, New York 10036.*

PRINTED IN THE UNITED STATES OF AMERICA

RAD 0 9 8 7 6 5 4 3 2 1

For my father
and my mother

# QUASAR

# 1

The holographic torso of a beautiful woman hung in the darkness of Theodore Karmade's tiny apartment. Her tangled black hair and black eyes were vivid against her pale skin, and she wore a black band around her neck.

"You lied to me," she said. Her voice was hoarse, throaty, and as she started to talk her supercilious smile dissolved into sweat like tears on her face. "You're a liar, like the rest of them. You *promised*. But you're going to deliver. You promised to take me, and you will.

"You don't remember because my aunt's people put a memory block on you. I'm sending a release sequence. Look straight at me."

The holoscreen went blank; then shapes and sounds avalanched around Karmade.

"A Mr. Ernest Qorndt, your most recent client, a high official in the ExoCity Mining Guild, has provided a very unfavorable reference for you," said the elegant, intricately figured Genanon Employment Agency logo hanging in the bright air of Karmade's VR garden. Unfocused bees buzzed sleepily over bright red and yellow flowers by the blurry stone wall. It looked pretty frowsy; Karmade wished he had had time to adjust the holo projector, but the want ad had only given him a few minutes notice for the job interview.

"Oh, Qorndt." Karmade cleared his throat. He could feel the sleep-tousled licks of hair he had combed down seconds before the interview standing up on his head in the hot ersatz sunlight. "I—he wanted some psych programming on his daughter I just couldn't do. Ethics code and so on."

"I'm sorry, I must have misunderstood you," said the logo, its cursor blinking calmly. "Our background inquiries of your Guild of Psychiatric Professionals disclose that Mr. Qorndt's deprogramming request fell within ethical guidelines."

Karmade's mouth felt dry. He should have guessed that an exclusive agency like Genanon would run that down—especially on a job with a salary like this one.

There was a long pause. A red lozenge glowed at the bottom of the logo, indicating that Genanon was doing a brain field scan. It had been there for the whole interview. Whatever the job was, they were interested in his brain functioning.

"Mr. Qorndt believes your initial delays and then refusal to deprogram his daughter led to her elopement with an undesirable person," the logo went on finally, "whereas prompt action on your part would have made it possible for her to return home. He told us he did not initiate proceedings to have your Psychiatric Technician's license revoked only because of a desire to avoid degrading publicity."

"That right?" mumbled Karmade. So instead he blackballed me, he thought bitterly. He waited stiffly for the logo to tell him that his application would remain on file and vanish from his apartment, as they all had for the past month. But instead there was another pause.

Then the logo said politely, "Mr. Karmade, I am pleased to inform you that your employment application has been accepted. Contract and other formalities will be concluded when you arrive at the work location. Thank you for your attention and congratulations on your success." By the time Karmade could close his mouth far enough to ask a question, the logo had blinked out.

Mystified and a little shaken, he stood up and switched off the holographic garden, the suddenly solid walls of his three-meter-square apartment giving him a familiar moment of claustrophobia.

A knock came at the door.

That was odd. He hadn't buzzed anyone through the gate to the floor's residential quadrant. Probably a mistake or a neighbor wanting to borrow something.

He slid the door open.

Karmade was a big man, still in good shape despite his forty years, but the two men in the hall were bigger. They both wore grey suits. One held out an ID card.

"Mr. Karmade?" he rumbled. "We're here to take you to the job you just accepted. See, it's a rush job, sir."

Vendors, idlers, and dusty factory workers just up from their shifts on the lower floors spared Karmade a moment of dull curiosity as the big men in grey escorted him through the metal gate separating his residential quadrant from the eightieth-floor mall area. As he hurried a step ahead of them, he half wondered if he was under arrest. Yet they hadn't coerced or threatened him, just urged him politely to hurry.

At first he thought they were taking him to the main building transvators, but they passed those, steered him to a narrow, grimy passageway off the central gallery. The passageway led to a door marked EMERGENCY that clicked open as if it knew the grey men's brain waves. Two more big, grey-suited men waited in the airlock beyond, one of them talking quietly into a headset. The second slid back a heavy door for Karmade and his escorts. Beyond, the bare concrete of an emergency landing bay opened on the toxic outer air, a private car filling it with the booming of idling rotors. Private use of an emergency bay was against City regulations, Karmade knew. He stopped short apprehensively.

"Please step on board, sir," said one of the men who had brought him. "We've been asked to transport you to your work location in a hurry."

"But who—who—" Who was important enough to arrange an escort like this, break City regulations—?

"Sorry, sir, I'm not allowed to say. But it's legitimate, I can tell you that."

The rotor-car, though luxurious, was closed, so Karmade couldn't see the building they landed in. From the bay where he disembarked, smelling of oil and roaring with the sound of rotors, one of the men in grey led him through an airlock and down a passage. At the end was an airtight door that hissed open. Inside was a Level 3 decon portal—a shower stall between two airlocks.

"I'll have to ask you to give me your clothes here, and all your personal effects," his escort said to him. "You'll be supplied with fresh items after you shower, Mr. Karmade. You're entering a Class A controlled environment, so you have to be decontaminated."

"A Class A environment?"

"Yes, sir. Please undress, Mr. Karmade. The quicker you decon, the quicker we can get you to your client. We're in an urgent situation, sir, so please help us by showering right away."

After a second of dumbfounded silence, Karmade started to tug at his clothes. The man helped him.

*A Class A controlled environment*— Most City residential buildings tried to maintain a Class C biocide toxicity level; the streets were Class D, and some swanky private residences were Class B. But Class A—that was reserved for the L-5 colonies and a few DNA banks hidden away behind millions of tons of concrete and steel deep in the City center, and—

Finished undressing, Karmade stepped into the shower stall. The man in grey politely took his watch and closed the door behind him. It hissed with pressure lock, and then hot, soapy water hit him from nozzles in the walls and ceiling. He took a sponge from a recess and began to scrub.

He felt shriveled in the hot water before some sensor was apparently satisfied with his contamination level and switched the shower off. Airjets dried him as he tried to figure out which of the few City Class A environments he could be in, wondering who had brought him here, and what in the world they could want him—a tech-grade psych operator—to do.

The airjets died and the stall's inner door hissed open. The inner airlock was a small dressing room. Clothes hung there: a discreet black business suit with fashionable black boots and black turtleneck, more expensive than anything he could have afforded.

"Please hurry, Mr. Karmade," a voice made him jump. "This assignment is urgent. Please put on the clothes." It wasn't the man in grey; this voice was sharp, wry, ironic.

Karmade was shivering despite all the hot water and hot air. "What *is* the assignment? I think I'm entitled—"

"A time-critical life or death situation, Mr. Karmade. Please hurry."

The clothes fit as if they had been made for him. As soon as he had fumbled them on the final airtight door hissed open and he was facing something he didn't at first recognize.

It was a hall, but so wide that the opposite wall was thirty meters away. He stepped hesitantly into it, boots clicking on a pink marble floor. He looked lengthwise down the hall and got dizzy.

It was all of pink stone and prodigiously long; it dwindled almost to nothing with distance in both directions, pillars of crimson marble rising to a lofty arched ceiling at hundred-meter intervals. It was lit gently from nowhere.

It had to be holographic. There was no place in the City this big, except perhaps—

"Mr. Karmade?"

The man stood only a dozen meters away but in all that hugeness his wiry figure had been swallowed up. He was dressed like Karmade in a black suit. He had a long, bony face with a hint of sour humor, a thin nose, long, disorderly white hair. His thin lips moved in a sardonic smile as he walked forward. The hand that shook Karmade's was bony and strong.

"Tom Rothe," he said. "We need to hurry, Mr. Karmade."

He made a polite gesture with one hand and conducted Karmade gently along with the other, their feet tapping rapidly. It seemed to Karmade that they could walk forever in that hall and not get anywhere. His stomach was jumpy with the expectation of learning what his new job was—and it had to be something bigger than he could have imagined, from the look of this place—

"I'm ZantCorp Sentrex Security Manager, Mr. Karmade, and we called you—"

*"Sentrex?"*

Rothe winced a little and kept Karmade walking with his gentle, steely hand. "We have to move quickly, Karmade; we're in an emergency situation and we need your immediate help. Please try to contain your surprise and respond as professionally and rapidly as possible—" Karmade's mind was racing. *Sentrex.* Somebody in the ZantCorp Sentrex Complex, the largest of the City's megastructures and headquarters to the corporate alter-ego of the City's wealthiest and most powerful Great Family, had hired him. Even if it was a low-level clerical position, the prestige of such a job would guarantee him an impeccable résumé, and Qorndt be damned.

Rothe took a text display from his jacket and folded it open in front of Karmade. A contract lit up on its screen.

"We need you to print this first," he said, pointing to the thumbprint square.

Karmade took the display, tried to concentrate on its words as he walked.

It was a kind of contract he had worked under a few times before: an agreement to act as the personal neuro-psychological caregiver of an incompetent subject. The terms were standard: he would use his best efforts and exercise the highest level of professional skill to ensure the safety and psychological health and well-being of the subject; he would act in all ways in the subject's interest and be bound by fiduciary obligations; he would undertake to protect the subject from all hazards, whether caused by animate or inanimate instrumentalities or by herself, to the best of his ability, etc.; but when he scrolled to the paragraph where the incompetent's name was inserted into the contractual jargon he actually stumbled on the slick marble floor.

It couldn't be.

"Zant?" he rasped as soon as he was able. "Quasar Zant?"

"You're disappointing me, Karmade," said Rothe. "Your psych profile led us to believe you'd cope better than this."

"But—" Why not hire one of the big psychiatric firms that specialized in care for disturbed rich individuals, and any of which Quasar Zant could buy outright with her enormous fortune? "But—doesn't she have psych care?"

"I'm in a hurry, Karmade," Rothe said. "My instructions are either you sign the contract or we give you a ride back home." He touched the scrolling panel, exposing the clause titled Salary. Karmade's eyes popped at the huge numbers, much bigger even than anything the want ad had mentioned.

"The offer lapses in thirty seconds," said Rothe. "You want to go back to your cozy little Guild, okay—except our sources say they're getting ready to expel you under pressure from some big shot. Twenty seconds."

"Qorndt!"

"That sounds like the name. He wants to see you go down to the sewer tribes, it seems. Ten seconds."

By law you were supposed to have a chance to examine the subject before you signed anything—

"Five seconds."

Karmade pressed his thumb onto the print square until the display beeped.

Rothe switched it off. He abruptly changed the direction they were walking, steering Karmade toward a crossing hallway that was relatively small: only ten meters across and two stories high. Its carpet was dark figured green, the walls paneled to head height with what looked like *real wood*, colonnades meeting at the vertex of the arched ceiling. It ended a hundred meters down at a big, arched door sunk into an alcove.

Rothe led Karmade into the alcove. Nothing happened for a few seconds: then there was a faint click and half a meter of armor under wood veneer slid silently aside. The pause had been for the door to read their brain fields, Karmade guessed, and if that was true it meant they had his field pattern on file—

Rothe stood to one side and gestured politely. "You go straight on."

Karmade looked at him in confusion, then a sudden dizzying panic. *Quasar Zant*— "What do you—?"

"Your patient is inside. Just go straight on and you'll see her."

"Aren't— Isn't—?"

"Please hurry, Mr. Karmade. As I told you, it's a matter of life or death. Please hurry."

He fairly shoved Karmade through the doorway, and it slid shut over his tense face.

Inside was a short entranceway and then a room— though "room" was the wrong word for it. Karmade stopped dead, squinting. In all the population-constricted spaces of the City—the narrow shops, tiny apartments, crowded, roofed streets—there was nothing like this. It was a space so big he didn't think he could see the opposite wall, though he might have been mistaken, since the wall behind him was barely recognizable as such: it was holographed to look like a screen of arches opening into fantastic vistas of courtyards and gardens, so realistic that the strange creatures and humans looking in from some of them made him jump. The room itself was a vast landscape of white pillars ranged along a veined emerald-green marble floor smooth and shiny as glass, so big that perspective made the white ceiling look low enough to bang your head on. Though it must be night by now, natural-looking sunshine splashed down from skylights. Everything was silent, still.

Karmade's mind raced in circles. His reality-testing faculty had been disrupted by the wildly implausible situational frame, he guessed: his sudden presence in the fabled Sentrex Complex; Security Manager Rothe's insistence that he, a tech-grade psych operator, rush to work on a life-or-death matter; but most of all, the fact that he had purportedly been hired to treat *Quasar Zant,* the richest and most glamorous person in the City.

He went back to the door to get more details from Rothe. The door didn't move.

He tried to concentrate, think logically. The situation could be a setup or illusion, though how or why such a thing should have been arranged he couldn't guess. Yet for all he could tell, this *was* ZantCorp Sentrex, or at least a place that could pass for it as far as he was concerned.

There was only one way to find out for sure. He smoothed his hair, trying to compose his face, which he guessed must look wild.

He started to walk into the room.

He walked a hundred meters in the silence, his boots clicking on the marble floor. The place was a playroom, he saw, with gargantuan toys. There were circus rides, including a roller-coaster extending high up into hollows in the white ceiling. There was an elaborate TV studio, complete with inert android actors on sound stages. There was an interplanetary space flight command station with computers and a huge planetarium

display, a boxing ring with a couple of eight-foot re-
mote-controlled gladiator robots, a sand desert holographed to look endless, with age-pocked stone
pyramid entrances in the foreground, and other play-
things ranged in every direction as far as Karmade could
see. He had walked about half a kilometer when he came
to what he guessed was a bed, nestled between an exo-
City mining rig simulator and a hundred-meter swim-
ming pool of still blue water. The bed was a cubic fifteen
meters of sleeping spaces at different levels connected by
stairs, ladders, and elevators, with built-in shelves, lamps,
closets, showers, whirlpool baths, food vendors, massage
machines, neuraudio equipment, and VR skins.

A young woman was standing in front of the bed.
She was the only person in the whole huge room, as far
as Karmade could see. She stood with her feet apart,
arms stretched over her head as if taking applause for a
perfect floor exercise at the Olympics. Her eyes were
closed, her nightshirt plastered to her body with milky,
oily sweat. She shuddered in waves.

Karmade shuddered too. Of course he knew the Intimate Secrets of Her Private Life the same way everyone
else did: the TV gossip columns often featured Quasar
Zant, Orphaned Mega-Trillionaire Pervo-Baby Jazzing
at the Exclusive Vibration Club, or Naughty Q.Z.'s
Electro-Neural Addiction Slaked in Sleazy 49th Quadrant 'Droid Palace. But there had always been the mel-
ancholy comfort, shared with millions of other viewers
in their tiny apartments, that the vertiginous possibilities
of her life, her searing beauty, the frightening insanity
that had caused so many delicious scandals, were all un-
alterably remote from him, as remote as the stars in the
sky.

Wires ran from a headset on her tangled raven-black
hair. They were attached to a console with a single flashing red light, mounted above a large, sunken sleeping
space in the huge bed. The console was cheap, crude,
the kind you could find in sleazy 'dromes and bars all
over the City. There had been sophisticated versions

once, with neural interfaces, but the Mutant Control Regulations had made the surgical modifications needed for the interface hardware illegal, and now there were only these primitive whole-brain induction drivers that damaged as many functions as they enhanced.

Other headsets, for shared-trip transductions, dangled from the console.

"Shit," hissed Karmade. He stepped close to her, heart pounding. *Quasar Zant*— He peeled up an eyelid fouled by puslike secretions. There was nothing but white; her iris was rolled all the way up into her head.

"Shit," he said again. Agitated, he climbed into the bed and stood on the sunken mattress, looked at the transducer readouts.

The level and scope of stimulation was incredible; almost every part of her brain was entrained in a jagged waveform he had never seen before, at 75 millivolts. The stimulation chronograph stood at 20.33 hours.

Maximum safe stimulation time for hypothalamic transducers was considered to be about four hours.

Panic blared in him. He scrambled off the mattress and gave Quasar Zant a quick examination with sweat-slick hands. Her skin was cold, clammy, greyish, her pulse and breathing barely detectable. She might already be dead, he realized, the pounding rhythms of the transducer keeping up a counterfeit of life as they rammed through her medulla, driving her autonomic systems.

He stared at her a moment longer, then turned and ran back toward the entrance door, boots clattering. He was halfway there when Tom Rothe's torso appeared in front of him.

He almost fell stopping.

"You bastard," was all he could gasp at Rothe. "You bastard."

Rothe looked at him bitterly. "Not my fault, Karmade."

"You're her security chief! You're responsible for her safety!"

Rothe smiled humorlessly, taking a text display from his pocket. "No. You are."

Karmade's heart deafened him. Suspicion was turning to cold fear in his stomach.

Rothe was talking as if to keep himself under control. "Ms. Zant expressed a wish to go to the Warrens," he said. "Her guardian said no. Ms. Zant doesn't like people saying no. She evaded our security surveillance somehow; by the time we realized she was on the 'ducer, she'd already been on too long for us to drag her off. What can you do for her?"

"Nothing. *It's too late.* Anybody pulls that headset off her she'll die."

"She can still do a voluntary, can't she? If she decides to take it off herself?"

"Theoretically. If she can still think. If she's still alive."

"She left us a note," said Rothe. "Said she'd get off voluntarily if we promised to take her to Death Hole Warren."

"You stupid bastard, you can't promise her anything anymore. Her senses are shut down by that machine, don't you understand? The only way to talk to her would be to put on one of the share headsets, but after twenty hours buildup the wave amplitude would kill you."

Rothe's mouth twisted in his humorless smile again, and his eyes were steady on Karmade.

"Oh, no," Karmade snarled. "You need a sucker to take the fall when she dies? Try your expedited hiring practices on someone else. I resign."

"I don't remember any such practices." Rothe patted the text display. He let that sink in, then went on. "I'll tell you something else, Karmade. We read your brain waves pretty good while you were talking to that phony want ad. If anybody in the City can get on the 'ducer with her, it's you. Your brain patterns are similar to hers, see? That's why we picked you. Field pattern coherence, the psych people call it. If anybody can get

her off the machine without damage, it's you. Just remember to tell her you'll take her to Death Hole Warren."

He flicked a finger through a holoswitch and disappeared.

Karmade stared at the place where he had been. His
mind was whirling again but things suddenly made
sense. He was probably a liability to the Psych Guild
now with Qorndt after him; someone expendable, a
loner without colleagues or friends; someone who could
be jailed for criminal malpractice while those responsible
went free—

And his only way out was to get Quasar Zant off the
transducer without killing her—or himself.

He cursed himself, feeling sick, the feeling of a man
about to commit suicide.

He went back to the huge bed and tore a sheet from
the sunken mattress. He tore a long strip off the sheet,
folded it with shaky hands, and wrapped it around his
head. That should weaken the transducer's current a little.

He picked up one of the share headsets and squeezed
his eyes closed, sweat running down his face.

He jammed the headset onto his head.

There was pain, searing, incinerating pain, as if someone was burning his head off with a flamethrower. He
tried to ride it, knowing it would tear him apart if he
fought it.

In a few minutes the pain ebbed and to Karmade's
astonishment he could see again. He was still standing in
the enormous, bright, silent room.

But Quasar Zant was gone.

He looked around. She was nowhere to be seen. He
was on the transducer by himself.

There was a sound—a sharp *crack*.

The emerald-green marble where Quasar Zant had
stood split open and caved in, cracks propagating rapidly

until the floor under Karmade splintered too and gave
way, and he fell—

—in a lacerating, choking tumble of rock and dust,
down through a dark hole into the rocky earth itself,
falling until he was terrified he would come out in the
Warrens among the mutants.

But instead he fell into someplace worse.

It was like Hell, a place of pain: electrocution and
incineration and suffocation all at once. He tried to
scream but there was no air; yet there was a sickening
smell and a horrible shrieking.

In electronic haze a figure writhed and struggled. It
was a representation of Quasar Zant, a snowman with
coal eyes and hair, a screaming mouth of running blood.
It writhed to free itself from tendrils of the static haze
that filled the place. The haze seemed to be alive: its
tendrils wrapped the Quasar-creature; where they
touched flame and smoke went up. The creature's body
was already covered with hideous, bone-deep burns. As
it yanked against the tendrils they snapped and evaporated, but more crept from the haze to wrap around it,
and Karmade could see that before long the Quasar-
creature would be dead.

Searing pain sliced across his own body. Burning tendrils were beginning to curl around him too, a hallucinatory representation of the transducer overload. He
screamed with fear and pain, and the horror that comes
when there is no escape. For he had no idea now how to
get off the 'ducer; he couldn't feel his body and had no
idea how to control it; he had entered Quasar's transducer trip and was as cut off from the outside world as
she was.

Out of the corner of his eye he caught a glimpse of
something standing next to him, something huge and
metal-golden, but when he yanked his shrieking face
toward it all he saw was an eye, a giant, unblinking Eye
floating in the haze like a logo.

"Call her," the Eye said calmly to him. "Call her by
name."

When its voice sounded, the incredible pain of the transducer was momentarily wiped out.

"Call her by name," said the Eye. "Say 'Quasar.' 'Quasar.' "

"Quasar!" It came out of his mouth burbling and distorted in the boiling haze. "Quasar!"

The burning snow-creature seemed to pause in its struggle, and Karmade felt the touch of someone's consciousness in the quasi-telepathic way the 'ducer allows.

"Tell her to get off the machine," said the Eye.

"Get off the machine! You're on a transducer, do you remember? Get off!"

The haze tendrils curled around the Quasar-thing like maggots, covering it with their writhing, worming bulk, boiling it into a featureless mass of death.

It erupted with screams like a geyser of blood, thrashing with insane agony.

"Call her," said the Eye. "Call her."

"You want to go to the Warrens?" screamed Karmade, the respite of the Eye's voice letting him remember what Rothe had said. "I'll take you there! I'll take you to the Warrens if you get off the 'ducer, you understand? The Warrens, you hear?" He thought the Quasar-thing paused again, and he felt again the touch of its mind.

"Tell her how to get off. Tell her to use her hands."

"You remember where your arms are, your hands? Can you feel them? Lift them up and take off the headset. Do you hear me, Quasar? Lift your hands up to your head and pull off the headset. Right now! Right now, and I'll take you to the Warrens! Right now! *Your hands! Now!*"

He didn't know how to do this himself, he realized, but at that moment someone took hold of his hands and squeezed them—squeezed them so that he remembered suddenly where they were. Then whoever it was lifted his numb arms and helped him clumsily rub his hands up the sides of his head. At the last second he caught another glimpse of the Eye; and then the flat, flaying light of the Hell-place and the fiery pain and the deafening beat of the neuroentrainment that he had been somehow unaware of until this second began to ebb away, and the vast Sentrex room faded back into view, silent and bright.

Quasar Zant stood in front of him again, her hands very shakily and weakly and clumsily scrabbling at the sides of her head. Karmade staggered to her and helped her, using her icy hands to push the headset slowly off. It left a bright red mark on her forehead. Her eyes opened a little. They were swollen and sticky, cocked off in different directions.

She fell heavily to the floor, headset clattering onto the smooth marble. Karmade fell too, on his hands and knees, and vomited—warm, acidic liquid filling his sinuses, splashing on his hands. He was lucky to be alive, he realized through nausea and shock; thank God for that talking Eye-thing, which he guessed had been his projection of the part of his own brain that could still think, remember, reason—

But who had helped him pull off his headset?

Voices and movement made him look up; people were suddenly all around. One of them pointed something at him; it made a small noise and pain flicked his side. As he fell forward into his pool of vomit, just before everything went black, he saw Tom Rothe standing over him with a sour smile.

# 2

Theodore Karmade stood in the darkness of his apartment, heart pounding, Quasar Zant's torso glowing in the air above his holo projector. Her face was pale, but not the death mask he had seen in the Sentrex bedroom. The curves of its lips and black eyes, the lines of the jaw and small, straight nose, sent a rush of serotonin-mediated disturbance through him.

"You remember now," she said, her voice soft and throaty and harsh, like a drug. "You remember what you promised. I've made an appointment for you at Hak Lun Associates in the 9th Sector tonight. Go there. But don't tell anyone. If my aunt finds out—" She licked sweat off her lips. "Go there," she said. "Or I'll make sure I die this time."

She disappeared with a flash of static, and Karmade's dingy apartment whirled around him in the dark.

"Ted, your reality testing faculty is excellent, and I applaud you for seeking a consultation regarding your hallucination," said the apartment psych expert system as Karmade combed his hair in his sanitary closet mirror. "The 'woman' you 'saw' on your console a little while ago may have been part of an acute delusional episode, with perhaps an organic etiology involving your sleep medication or some tainted food; or she may have been a hypnotic construct transmitted by one of the psycho-vandalism groups that news reports say have gained illegal access to large blocks of private TV addresses over the past months. Certainly the idea of the City's richest familycorp hiring you to save a notorious beauty from suicide has strong infantile wish-fulfillment elements, which you yourself have recognized." The psych system had programmed itself over a number of years to respond to psychological data just as Karmade would himself, saving him the time it took to think out diagnoses in routine cases.

"But the new memory chain seems *real,* while the one where the money in my account is a bonus for deprogramming the Qorndt girl seems hazy and insubstantial, obviously faked," countered Karmade, straightening his turtleneck and adjusting his jacket. He studied the face in the mirror for a moment—still good-looking, but showing signs of stress around the eyes and in the creased forehead. He felt dizzy and confused, bothered by a headache and a pain in his side that the now vague memory slug said was from where he had fallen in the shower a week ago.

"As you know, Ted, hallucinations can seem more real than actual events when—"

He flicked a finger through a lozenge of red light in the air, switching the expert off. Yet on his way to the subway level in the crowded building transvator, fear flared in him. If the new memory chain *was* real, it meant ZantCorp had memory-blocked him on the services he had rendered to Quasar Zant, probably to kill any possible publicity. And if ZantCorp had memory-blocked him, it meant ZantCorp wanted him to forget; and ZantCorp wasn't an organization you defied. That he was even thinking of defying it had to do with the serotonin reward associated with Quasar Zant's face and voice, he guessed, and the fantasy elements of being summoned by the City's most infamous society goddess, as his psych system had recognized.

Yet she *was* the central personage at ZantCorp, he reminded himself, despite her mental problems; if she really had called him, he didn't see how ZantCorp could object to his coming. It would be safer to stay at home, of course, but—the thought of passing up a chance to meet Quasar Zant again brought a depression over him even more potent than his fear of ZantCorp.

He had been steered into psychiatric technology by his school aptitude tests and his relatively high IQ—it had been either study psych tech or lose the post-secondary slot his test scores had won him. But he had never liked it; he would rather have been a Boundary Guard or an exominer, or almost anything else, he sometimes thought. While his fantasies of changing professions had faded after he graduated from the Psych Guild technical school and settled down to oversee a dozen AI psych-booths and—after he got more seniority—take on a private caseload, he still kept up an expensive VR Safari Club membership to keep a little excitement in his life. Maybe he needed excitement.

He would act out the Quasar Zant fantasy cautiously, he told himself as the crowded transvator car made gravity coming to a rapid halt at the subway level; he would just go see what it was all about, if anything. He could always go home if things started to look dangerous.

From its 9th Sector location and the bland anonymity of its street front, Karmade guessed Hak Lun Associates was one of those posh clinics that treated the mutant viral infections no amount of City legislation could keep from seeping up out of the Warrens. That kind of place was often disguised as a health club or doctors' office, with tight security so that wealthy sufferers could get treated without losing face or their jobs. The 9th Sector meant no neon or crowds, just clean, empty galleries kept at a neutral temperature and holographed with bushes and lawns in somber nighttime colors, echoing with the simulated creaking of crickets. The galleries emerged at intervals into twenty-story atriums that the upper-class residential blocks rose through, skylights showing them towering into the night sky beyond. Karmade knew private police were employed to keep the undesirable element out of neighborhoods like this, but none of them seemed to be around as he stood under Hak Lun Associates' plain, lighted portico and let the entrance hardware read his brain. There was no sign that Quasar Zant, Non Compos Mentis Mega-Trillionaire, was in the vicinity either.

Hak Lun's heavy street door clicked and rolled aside. Karmade's heart hammered. His palms were wet. So some aspects, at least, of his new memory chain were real. He stepped into the small transvator behind the door.

The 'vator took him up to the 107th floor without being asked. At the end of a featureless hallway another door slid aside to reveal a small waiting room with burgundy carpet and wallpaper, imitation wood chairs and an antique vase on a stand. There was a tone, and a pleasant female voice said, "Welcome to Hak Lun Viral Associates, Mr. Karmade. Please step through door A. If you need assistance, be seated and a sentient technician will arrive in a few minutes." Door A was outlined discreetly by a strip of violet light. It slid aside and he went into a cubicle with a stool and a headset on a white table.

"Please sit down and put on the headset," said the voice. "We will take a history first."

He hadn't figured out why Quasar Zant or someone impersonating her would want him to undergo screening for a mutant viral infection, but the headset was a different story. When the AI voice started giving him a series of standard psych tests—including the ones for memory block and lie-detector avoidance programming —he guessed that Hak Lun Viral Associates was in turn a cover for something else, perhaps something with an even more tenuous legal status. Soon the voice asked him straight out whether he was a police or media agent. And after that he wasn't surprised when another violet-outlined door appeared in the wall with a logo that said, "Hak Lun's Dusk House."

Karmade had heard of the exclusive bioenvironment clubs that catered to the City's richest citizens and were kept secret to prevent public unrest; but he was stunned anyway when he stepped into a place too big to measure, extended by holography so that there was no way to tell where the real gardens ended and the simulated landscape began. It was as beautiful as the most idyllic VR garden in the Public Library files—full of deep evening light, with overgrown beds of flowers and bushes, streams, trees, and graveled walks stretching on and on through a rolling landscape—but this was *real*, maintained at unimaginable expense on soil and water enriched with the primordial nutrients the vegetation needed to grow, cleansed of the biocides that had stained the planet ever since the survivors of the biowars had destroyed the ecological cycles in the process of killing off the leftover hypermutagenic viruses. Among the trees were flickering candles in bowers of dusk, and laughing voices rippled faintly in the still, warm air. High in the evening sky a sickle moon shone.

As Karmade stood gawking a volume of air near him glowed and hummed with the mysterious, twanging music in fashion those days, and a man who had not been there before stepped out of it. He wore a silver-grey tuxedo. He took in Karmade's suit for a millisecond, then said, "Your accommodation is ready, Mr. Karmade. This way please."

Their feet crunched on gravel. Karmade felt numb and elated, probably from the psychoactive chemicals he knew they pumped into the air in places like this. As they rounded some trees a column of light came into view. He suddenly lurched off the path toward it, breath catching in his chest.

It was a transparent cylinder two meters in diameter

and four tall, full of water with lights shining through it. There was something alive in the water, something with enormously long legs, clouds of golden hair floating about its head. Something seven feet tall and bone-thin, with three sets of breasts and webbing between its fingers and toes. When it saw Karmade looking it swam down and put its hands where his were on the glass. A breathing mask covered its nose and mouth. Its blue eyes were slanting and hypnotic. There were four of them.

"We call her Glinda," said the tuxedoed man behind Karmade. "As far as we know she is the only one in existence. Her bones are so soft she can only live in water."

The thing stared into Karmade's eyes. There was a death sentence for harboring mutants on the surface, so she had to be counterfeit—a holographic projection, an android, or even a half-starved human actress with prostheses—but she looked real. Karmade found himself wondering just how far outside the law a place like Hak Lun's might go to give its rich patrons a thrill.

He tore himself away from the eyes. The man led him among more trees and down into a sudden little dell where the damp, intoxicating smell of vegetation was strong. They seemed all at once alone, out of sight of the candles, out of earshot of the talk and laughter. There was a rock face jutting from the steepest side of the dell, bushes and vines growing up it. Karmade's guide pushed aside some of the vines and held them awkwardly. Behind them was a little grotto or cave, just high enough to stand in. The opening the held vines made was big enough for Karmade to slip through at the tuxedoed man's nod. His heart was hammering again with suspense in spite of the psychoactive aerosols. He tried to ask whether Quasar Zant was meeting him here, but the man had let the vines down again and his footsteps were crunching away along the path. Karmade stood in the faint light with his hand on one wall to keep his footing on the uneven floor, trying to see out. The rock around him was dusty, flaky, and veined, as if a real cave had somehow grown in the heart of this downtown skyscraper. Karmade guessed it had been cut out whole from some hillside in the barren exoCity, decontaminated, and brought here in one piece.

There was a hum and the cave rotated, almost throwing him to the floor.

When it stopped, the faint sounds of the garden had disappeared, replaced by flat silence. The cave opening now faced inward, 180 degrees from where it had been. Karmade stared through it at rough, grey concrete stairs that went down into darkness. A human skull lay on the top stair.

"Hello?" he said. There was no answer.

After a minute he hesitantly stepped out onto the top stair.

With a heavy rasping a wall rolled into place behind him, leaving him in pitch-darkness. He pushed on it but it didn't move. He guessed that the hidden cave in Hak Lun's Dusk House, alias Hak Lun Viral Associates, and disguised even under that name, had rotated back to its original position. Since the Dusk House was probably a place only a few people in the City knew, these stairs, kept secret even from the usual patrons, must be something really special.

And in such places, he guessed, Quasar Zant might be found.

From a great distance—far, far away down many hundreds of stairs—a faint, tormented wail sent an icy trickle through him.

It took him a long time after that to start down into the dark.

The stairs wound down a long way. After a few dozen a sickly glow seemed to come from the concrete walls and ceiling that pressed narrowly around him. A movement of cold air from below brought a smell like something kept too long in the refrigerator. Here and there mausoleumlike stone doors were set in the walls, and dimly through one of them Karmade thought he heard the monotonous creak of a rusty machine as he passed. In one place a monstrous mutant skeleton with a long, snaking spine, many clawed limbs, and a huge, quasi-human skull was stretched out along the stairs. He squatted to examine it, trembling. If this place was some kind of elaborate pervodrome, it catered to weird tastes.

A heavy, dull scraping came from below, and as he rounded the curve of the stairs Karmade saw one of the mausoleum doors swing inward, revealing a low, dark tunnel. He hesitated, then stooped inside.

The tunnel smelled even worse than the stairs, a rotting stench. The ceiling was too low to let him stand upright. The walls were worn stone, slimy with moss and oozing water.

A shape loomed in the dimness and Karmade leapt backward, hitting his head on the ceiling.

A decayed human body hung in shackles, its broken joints grotesquely twisted.

It was either go back or go past it. Karmade held his breath and slid along the opposite wall, shielding his face with his hands and fighting nausea.

Thirty meters on two more bodies hunched, this time on opposite sides of the tunnel so that there was no way past without touching them.

One of them lifted a hand and beckoned, rotten rags falling from its arm. Its face worked horribly.

"You can go on in, sir, after we search you," it said. "She's expecting you."

The other body got animated and the two of them shuffled expertly around Karmade with weapons detector wands, desiccated eyes intent on their work.

"OK, sir, go on through."

A little farther on the tunnel opened into a huge, dark canyon. Flames burned in a candelabra in the middle of it, making a flickering circle of yellow light. Karmade walked toward that, feet crunching on what looked like a solid floor of crumbling bones.

Someone crouched among the bones near the candelabra: a pale figure wearing rags. One smooth shoulder and what he could see of the legs were dirty with ashes, and ashes fell from the hair. The bare arms were circled by black medication bracelets. Balanced on the bones nearby was a tarnished silver tray with a glass of murky brown wine and some rotten-looking prototien that thumb-sized cockroaches swarmed over silently.

She didn't look at him. She stared into an open pit a meter away, where two dried skeletons lay. One of them wore the remains of a black tuxedo, the other the rags of a bridal veil.

Her lips worked silently. Finally she whispered, still not looking at him, "I'll go in there soon. You'll go too. Everyone goes into that hole."

Karmade found his voice somehow. It fell dead in the huge space. "It's not real, Ms. Zant. It's all made of plastic and plaster and serotonin antagonist precursors in the air to make you think you're having existential despair."

"It's real," she whispered. "We and everything we know are going to die, go away forever. Life is a little flash of light in the darkness that dies and is gone. *And we know it,* and that's what makes our lives a living death, like prisoners waiting for the executioner. The people we see are ghosts. I died before I was born. Everything is made of plastic and plaster and . . ."

"A course of norepinephrine and serotonin reuptake inhibitors—" Karmade started.

She was staring at him now, with dull hostility, her eyes dead black holes in a pale mask. Her voice was ashen. "Who are you?"

Karmade's palms were wet. "Ted Karmade. The psych tech you—you called—"

"Do they really think I'm that far gone? That I can't remember who I called or didn't call? I told them I was to be *left alone.*"

"But—you—"

"Go away. You go away or I'll scream. I'll have a fit. If you make me have a fit my aunt will have you killed and thrown in the garbage, even if she hired you to come here. Go away before I scream."

Karmade backed away from her, stumbling on the bones.

"I'll have a fit," Quasar Zant gasped, rocking back and forth, arms wrapped around herself, hands clutching at her rags. "I'll have a fit." She seemed to be unaware of him now, and he thought he saw a sudden sheen of sweat gleaming on her in the dim light.

Then, strangely, she seemed to change. Her eyes closed, then fluttered open, and she shuddered. Then her body straightened from its sick slump and a flush stole into her cheeks. Her delicate nostrils flared, and her eyes were like the eyes of someone who had just woken up.

She looked at Karmade.

And she disappeared. Karmade was looking straight at her; he saw the air around her turn strangely refractive, like a thickening liquid mirror that finally reflected perfectly, but in a way that let you see what was behind it instead of what was in front of it, and she was gone, swallowed into the dark landscape.

Then several things happened at once. A faint, odd prickling radiated from his waist and the candelabra light took on a silver tinge, like moonlight—Karmade guessed some kind of electromagnetic cloak had been thrown over him. Quasar Zant appeared out of thin air, and so did a dozen guards all around her, one close enough to touch. The guards' eyes were wide with surprise, and several were pulling guns from holsters. They groped toward Karmade and Quasar; apparently Quasar's cloaks were more powerful than their detectors.

Quasar grabbed Karmade's arm. "Run!" she hissed.

He ran wildly in the direction she dragged him, nearly falling in a tangle of plaster bones and rubber cadavers, knocking one of the guards down as he tried to keep his feet.

The guard's gun bouncing off a fake skull practically

jumped into his hand. He stuffed it reflexively into his
pocket.

In a moment they were in the entrance tunnel, but
one of the moldering corpses that had frisked Karmade
blocked it, gun outstretched. Quasar's shoulder hit it in
the midsection and it jackknifed to the ground. Karmade
stumbled on its head as he passed.

"Where are you—?"

They brushed the fake manacled corpse, raising a
stink that almost made Karmade unconscious. He staggered out the mausoleum door hitting his head, and
then she was dragging him down the concrete stairs so
fast his feet barely touched them, and into a small, battered freight elevator. There was a click of buttons and
the elevator was shooting downward.

Quasar Zant's body—slender and smooth but muscular as the extinct wild animals they showed sometimes
on TV, and not much hidden by the pervodrome rags—
was covered with sweat and heaving with breath. Her
small, high-arched feet left bloodstains on the floor. Her
hands clawed the elevator handrail, black eyes stabbing
at Karmade.

"Are you Karmade?" she gasped.

"I'm Karmade," he stuttered. "What's—what's happening here?"

"My father's cloaks," she said triumphantly, running
her hand over a heavy black belt resting on her hips,
covered with tiny controls and indicator lights. He had
one around his own waist too, Karmade realized suddenly. She must have put it on him back in the cavern
while she was invisible. "I can see you and you can see
me, but nobody else in the world can see either of us, no
matter what kind of detector they're using—unless
they're wearing one of these. And nobody else can get
one. My father never released this design to anyone, and
he only made half a dozen of them. Not even my aunt's
people know about them. On full cloaking they block all
sensory output—electromagnetic, audial, tactile, everything. Do you have a gun?"

"No I don't have a gun," he said, feeling the bulge in his pocket. He closed his eyes, took some deep breaths, and used an antiadrenergic mantra for half a minute, then tried to make a snap diagnosis. Probably some acute exacerbation of a hyperdopaminergic or bipolar syndrome, judging by her unusual strength and lack of obvious disorientation; yet if so it had come over her with a strange suddenness. He began to talk again, clearly and reasonably, using his best therapeutic manner: "You know where you are, don't you, Quasar? You're in a nightclub where your guardian sent you to have a good—"

She savagely knocked away the hand he was sliding toward the elevator control panel.

"There's no need to be afraid. There are people in this building who want to help you. They know ways to make you feel less upset, more like yourself. You'll be—"

"You're taking me to the Warrens."

"I'm not taking you to the Warrens." Fear interrupted his calm tone. He tried to relax again. "See, we both have a different idea of what's going on here, and we need just a few minutes to discuss it and straighten it out."

"We don't need to discuss anything. You're going to take me to Death Hole Warren, like you promised. If you don't, I'll tell my aunt's people you kidnapped me. I read your psych profile, the one my aunt used to hire you," she sneered. "You don't have the guts to face that."

The elevator made gravity and stopped with a final jerk. The readout said they were at the lowest subbasement level.

"They'll euthanatize you," she said. "Think about that."

The door trundled open to show a dim, humming hallway painted a flaking industrial green, a thick overhead pipe running along it as far as Karmade could see. Quasar gave him a sneer and ran.

He stood looking after her.

"Ms. Zant," he called when she was out of sight in the dimness. "Let's go back upstairs." His voice fell dead, not echoing at all, as if he stood in a tiny room full of cotton wool. Effect of the cloaking belt he realized, which cut off all sound he made.

A distant, terrified screaming answered him.

The hallway went on forever. Karmade was halfway down it, lungs bursting, when the screaming suddenly cut off.

Half a kilometer from the elevator the big pipe disappeared through an armored ventilation grating set into a blank wall with warning signs on it. The grating was ajar, as if somebody had pulled it hurriedly into place behind them.

He wrestled it open. It swung on hinges and hit the wall with a boom that throbbed back and forth through the hallway like a heartbeat.

"Ms. Zant?" he gasped.

Trembling with exertion and fear he climbed into the tunnel behind the grating. This subbasement might be far enough down to open into the Boundary Zone, and if it did— The tunnel was low, pitch-black, sour-smelling, the walls greasy soot under his hands. He was five meters in when a noise made him jerk around.

Someone was dragging the grating shut behind him.

By the time he scrambled back to her the three massive smart bolts on the grating had refastened themselves.

He stared at her in the dim light, stricken. Her face and shoulders were streaked with soot, and her tangled hair and crazy eyes made her look like a sewer tribe girl.

"You psychotic bitch," was all he could gasp, "the Maggots—!"

A remote vibration and a faint movement of air made him claw at the grating, heart hammering. It was unmoving, solid as stone.

He turned and slammed his back against it. "I'm not a mutant!" he shouted. "I was lured in here against my will—!"

With a faint scratching of its hundred metal legs on the floor and walls, a Maggot's blunt snout appeared from the blackness of the tunnel, four rubber humanoid heads rotating hideously on top of it.

Quasar Zant was smiling now and actually moving toward the Maggot—toward her death, since the Maggots were built to penetrate all known cloaking.

She put her hands on its corroded metal snout and kissed the nearest humanoid head, actually sticking her tongue into its dry rubber mouth as it rotated past.

Karmade was frozen. His breath was frozen. The Maggots were the machines the City used to guard the lowest level of sewers and utility tunnels, the zone between the surface and the underground shelter-city where the mutants lived, machines programmed to kill anything alive in the places they patrolled, to prevent contamination of the human race by the mutants the biowars had made. In a second this one would incinerate Quasar and him with its particle guns.

The Maggot hesitated, its modular android heads—which contained many of its sensors—continuing to rotate. Then, apparently satisfied that the noise it had detected had come from somewhere beyond the grating, it started to back up, its sectioned body withdrawing into the darkness of the tunnel with a clicking of mandibles, and in a few seconds it was gone.

Quasar turned to Karmade. There was a smudge on her lips where she had kissed the machine.

Karmade yanked at the grating again.

"Hey!" he screamed through the bars. "We're in here! We're in here!" His voice fell absolutely flat.

Quasar's voice was calm, reasonable. "No one can hear you. Come with me if you want to get out of here —remember, cloaking can't keep you from starving to death. Or you can take off the belt and it'll take about two minutes for that Maggot to find you."

She scrambled into the darkness of the tunnel.

Karmade scrambled after her, cursing wildly.

The tunnel was pitch-black, its dead, sour air burning his lungs. After a few hundred meters a faint grey glow opened above him. A rust-scaled ladder went up a concrete shaft; a dark, lithe shape was climbing it. He struggled up after her, and when he got to the top she was tapping the keypad on another grating.

A rising whisper in the space above the grating turned into a roar, and hot, electric-smelling air blew on them as something big rushed past.

The smart bolts snapped back and Quasar shoved the grating open, muscles rippling. She climbed up through the hole.

Karmade climbed after her. He was starting to be able to think again. However good her planning for this escape from ZantCorp security—and it had to be good for her to have the bolt combinations to these gratings, which were top-secret City information—she was obviously acutely decompensated, with delusions of omnipotence and grossly inappropriate affect. She could get herself killed on this romp, and if she did he guessed he would have a lot more to worry about than expulsion from the Psych Guild.

They were in a big concrete tunnel that smelled of oil, hot metal, and electricity. Bundled cables ran along the walls, a massive, T-shaped rail along the graveled floor. The rear car of a freight train was ten meters from them, a dim purple light glowing on it.

Quasar leapt lightly onto the wide top of the rail and climbed the dented metal of the car, clambered over the edge and out of sight.

The train was starting to lift up and move on its magnetic cushion when Karmade sprawled after her onto hard plastic ingots.

# 3

990th Street ran through the 77th Sector, an old, deep part of the City that the reconstruction programs hadn't gotten to yet. It was crowded and dimly lit, rising and falling in slopes and worn concrete steps that followed an ancient, now-invisible topography, roofed in places with cracked concrete, in others with corrugated metal or even plastic sheets that rattled in the rain that had started in the night, letting water drip through to run in poisonous rills people avoided along the worn pavement. Opposite a candy shop, its wares heaped on plastic trays under colored neon lights, two sanitation workers in dirty coveralls stood by a vending machine with a garish sign that advertised "Rooms—Weekly—Daily—Hourly."

They were arguing.

"Why are we stopping here?" the stocky, balding one said in a deep, gravelly voice. "You said you would take me—"

"I didn't say that," the other one, taller and thinner, snapped. "I said I wanted to talk about it. And I need a rest. I can't go any further without rest. Do you have any cash? All I have is debit, and they'll be monitoring transactions by this time."

The stocky one dug in his coveralls and came up with a coin.

"This is the smallest thing you've got?" said the tall one. "We don't need this place for a year."

"Yes."

Karmade shrugged and put it in a slot, took the flimsy plastic card the machine extruded.

The card opened a metal door in the seamed concrete wall behind the vendor, and they rode up thirty floors in a tiny, molded-plastic elevator with a malarial shudder and a smell of hot transformers. The door opened on a narrow hall with a stained rug and cheap, garish lumtiles in the ceiling. Their room was near the end, a two-meter cubicle almost filled up by a creaky, sagging bed, a sanitary closet opening at its foot, TV and vending machine set into the wall. There was no window. As soon as Karmade had the door bolted, the stocky sanitation technician melted into a mist of distorted reflections that evaporated in the lumtile light, depositing Dazzling Trillionaire Truant Quasar Zant, still in her pervodrome rags, into the sleazy dayroom with him.

She was greasy with sweat, streaked with soot and dirt, a scrape on her arm oozing blood, bruises darkening her knees. She tapped at a miniaturized keypad on Karmade's belt and his torn, filthy suit emerged from the sanitation tech's coveralls.

"What do you want to talk about?" asked Quasar.

Her eyes were suspicious, resentful, with a dizzy sleepiness in them. Karmade guessed somebody somewhere was broadcasting the signal that dumped neuroleptics and hypnotics from her remote-activated medication bracelets and choker necklace into her blood. More power to them. As soon as she went to sleep he would get on the TV to ZantCorp and tell them to come get her. He would make them understand that he had had to follow her from Hak Lun's to keep her from hurting herself. Hopefully they would be eager enough to avoid publicity to let it rest there; maybe they would even give him something for his trouble. Either way, he wished deeply that he had listened to his apartment psych expert and not let his infantile fantasies tempt him into getting mixed up with a dangerous psychotic.

"You OK?" he asked sympathetically, helping her to sit on the bed. "You want some water?" He got her a disposable cup of brownish liquid from the sanitary closet, noticing that he couldn't see himself in the mirror.

She made a face at the taste of the water. She slumped down on the pillow and her eyes closed, then opened, flickering around the room emotionlessly.

"People live in places like this?" she asked flatly.

"Whole families live in places like this. And lots worse places."

She closed her eyes again. "I told you what I'll do if you don't take me to Death Hole Warren. I want to go now."

"I'll take you," he said soothingly. "But I need a little while to rest, pull myself together. And I want to make sure you really want to go there. And to understand why."

"I need to find out something about myself," she mumbled, and let him take the cup out of her dirty hand.

"No need to go to the Warrens for that," he said with false heartiness. "Just watch the TV. They know all about you."

She looked at him as if trying to read his face. He got two lumpy pillows behind her head and threw part of the ashen-smelling bedspread over her, then said, "TV up."

Nothing happened.

Even though Quasar had removed their projected disguises, she had kept their cloaks on; the TV hadn't been able to hear him. He looked down at the intricate belt covered with superminiaturized hardware and tiny, strange displays. "How do you turn this thing off?"

She didn't answer.

There was a complicated mechanism by the buckle; after fumbling with it for a minute he figured out that you had to press two panels simultaneously with your thumbs. When he pressed them the tingling around his body went away and the belt vanished.

One second he had been holding it and then it was gone. He looked on the floor at his feet and then on the bed—and jumped. Quasar Zant was gone too. Not only that, but the bed was made, the cover he had thrown over her tucked neatly around the mattress again.

He stared, wondering if this was some kind of cloaking he had never seen before or if the delusion his psych expert had warned him about—only hours ago, though it seemed like days—had just resolved itself.

A haze on the bed thickened to liquid mirror and broke apart, showing Quasar Zant sitting in the again-rumpled cover. She had one hand on her belt controls.

"If you're going to turn on the TV, *hurry*," she said angrily. "They'll be doing a City-wide brain trace search for us." And she vanished, the bed making itself again. Apparently the cloaking belts not only hid their subject but broadcast a plausible cover scene to make it impossible to infer his or her presence.

"TV up," he said again, and when the holo menu was floating by his head, flicked a finger through GOSSIP and then ZANT, and studied the submenu that appeared:

QUASAR ZANT

1. Latest Antics        4. Legal Battles
2. Society Scandals     5. Glamorous Lifestyle
3. Fabulous Wealth      6. Background

He flicked a finger at 6. Something not too exciting to help lull her to sleep.

The room got dark. Then it was filled with a deep, portentous voice and a holographic aerial view of Zant Sentrex, gigantic and many-spired, the camera angle dwarfing the City below and around it.

"Behind the impenetrable walls of the famous Sentrex skyscraper, behind the armored legions, formidable financial empire, and the world's most feared private secret police, lies one of the most fascinating mysteries of our time. Quasar Zant! The name brings—"

There was a faint prickling, the light changed, and Quasar was kneeling next to him, a hand on his belt controls. A chill went through him at her closeness; the TV had reminded him who she was.

She slumped dully back onto the pillows.

"—only child of eccentric trillionaires Irneldo and Nova Zant." The TV showed two slender, black-haired people with dark sunglasses and black overcoats hustling through a crowd inside a wedge of security operatives. They looked more like brother and sister than husband and wife.

"Shown in this rare unreconstructed footage en route to City Court to justify controversial technological innovations, they were rarely photographed because of the advanced electromagnetic shielding devices, invented by the Zants themselves, that usually surrounded them.

"As one celebrity put it, everything about the Zants was peculiar, including the way they made their money and the way they died. In fact, both Irneldo Zant and Nova Cloud, who became his wife, were born penniless. As mated astronauts on the first Neptune Orbiter mission they were almost lost when their scout ship collided with an uncharted moonlet." An illuminated diagram of the solar system replaced the Zants. "Robots from the Orbiter rescued them, but the experience was traumatic. On their return to Earth four years later friends found them antisocial, introverted, scarcely recognizable. They resigned from the colonization program and, with the pay from their Neptune mission, started a small electronics business. Fourteen years later they were the richest people in the world.

"The richer they became, the more reclusive they became. Irneldo and Nova Zant seemed intent on using their money to devise ever more impenetrable hideaways for themselves and their only child, Quasar. Their wealth and power had reached their zenith when they purchased most of the City's central 164th Sector, razed the buildings, and constructed the Sentrex complex." The 164th Sector appeared spouting clouds of dust as buildings collapsed; then giant construction machines swung and lifted and rolled across the dirty bedspread. "Informed sources report that enormous gardens, forests, and orchards of natural biological organisms, seeded from the City's super-secret DNA bank, as well as unimaginably fabulous living spaces, were constructed within. Irneldo and Nova Zant and their baby daughter moved into this four-hundred-floor structure surrounded by legions of servants and security personnel, emerging only occasionally to testify in court proceedings. News of their deaths in a laboratory explosion reached the outside world six years later, sparking legal battles over control of their financial empire. Their orphaned daughter Quasar, now eight years old—"

There was a sob that didn't come from the TV. Karmade looked at Quasar. She was hunched in the bedspread, one arm curled over her tangled hair. Her face was intensely twisted with grief.

She was hot and sweating. If her medication jewelry was working right she was exhibiting a neuropharmacological transition to a sedated state.

"It's all right," Karmade said softly, adjusting her pillows. "Just relax. You're all right."

She convulsed with another tearing sob.

"I need them," she gasped. "There's something wrong with me, can't you see? They could help me. But they're gone."

Sympathetic somatic conversion, grief reaction type.

Gently, "Tell me why you think there's something wrong with you."

"Are you stalling me here until my aunt's people find us and take me back?"

He opened his mouth to produce a therapeutic evasion but now her wet, reddened eyes were raised to his, and he had a sudden, uncanny feeling: as if she had reached between his ribs and grabbed his heart, pressing it pitilessly in her slender hands to test its quality as one might press a slab of prototien to see if it was rotten.

He closed his mouth.

She slumped back on the bed suddenly, eyes rolling up in her head with what looked like sudden-onset kainate and quisqualate ion channel saturation.

He let out his breath with relief.

But as he turned to the TV to call ZantCorp he heard rather than felt the solid blow to the back of his head, followed by stars and splinters of light, and only then by red-hot pain, and then he was falling very slowly into black, listening as he went to the TV: ". . . adjudged incompetent by a City judge, who appointed her mother's sister, Nelda Cloud, as her guardian . . ."

Theodore Karmade had no training or experience as a hero; yet when he woke up on the greasy rug of the cheap 77th Sector dayroom, stomach heaving and head roaring, he knew that his life depended on what he did next. He had let a self-destructive psychotic escape from his custody under circumstances suggesting that he had kidnapped her, and she was probably headed to Death Hole Warren right now to get herself killed. That would be bad enough anytime, but in this case the psychotic was Quasar Zant, whose guardian practically ran the City.

He forced himself to sit up despite the pain in his head. Plastic packaging was strewn on the rug by the room vendor, labels indicating it had held a cheap jumpsuit and boots. His heart began to pound. Death Hole Warren was in the next Sector over—Quasar had even

managed to pick a freight train going near her goal—
close enough that by the time Karmade got through to
someone at ZantCorp and got them to understand what
was happening, she might already be there, in her cloak
nobody could see through. But if he got there before
her—and maybe he could, because he was used to travel-
ing in the City and she wasn't—he could grab her or get
the Boundary Guards to grab her—

1,036th Street was one of the deepest and oldest in
the City, its walls dark with ancient grime, the reek of
wet garbage mingling with the smells of food and spices
from tiny, cavelike shops. Karmade pushed invisibly
through the crowds below neon lights wired up under
the dripping plastic roof. At a corner a grizzled, blind
beggar sat on a step.

"Brothers and sisters," he mumbled, holding out
one swollen hand for coins. "Brothers and sisters, God
be with you."

Karmade pushed in a direction where there were
fewer people. After a few blocks there was a decon lock
with rusted turnstiles and a double set of dirty revolving
doors. Outside in the muddy exterior street the quiet
and emptiness were sudden and disorienting. Though
environmental conditions had improved in the past
twenty years, few people ventured outside the covered
streets, with their airlocks and decon systems, to avoid
building up dangerous levels of the biocides that still
stained the planet.

The only sound out here was a vast, diffuse throbbing of machinery, like the City's heartbeat. Above, the
roofless air went up dizzyingly into grey haze. The street
was dim, deserted except for an occasional Boundary
Guard sentinel in a tiny, sealed observation booth, and
the corrugated steel sheds packed with android soldiers
standing breathless and blank, waiting to be called out in
case of a mutant breakout, food riot, or other emergency. The rain had stopped but everything was wet,
dripping. Karmade ran, feet sucking in the mud, the

cloaking belt keeping him from tripping any detectors. A little farther on there were no more sheds or Guard booths. The sound of dripping water loomed large in the silence. Cement had been poured into the windows and doors of the buildings as far up as he could see, and the walls were plastered with peeling posters showing the Mayor's stern face and the words: "Remember! Mutants Mean Death: To Your City—To Your Race—To You!" And then he came to an alley.

The floor of the alley was mud, and in the mud, very clear and still filling with foul water, were the prints of small, new boots. Karmade squatted over one of them, heart pounding.

Then he lifted his head and looked thirty meters down the alley to the two-story metal gate. There was no time now to get ZantCorp security here, or even alert the Boundary Guards. By now she must be at the end of the primary tunnel, by the shafts where every month they took the mutants caught by the City's endless dragnets and genetic testing programs—

Karmade stood up shakily and wobbled forward. He felt sick. He stopped a couple of times and turned to run, but there was nothing to run to except a death sentence if he went back without her. Even so, it took the knowledge that he was wearing a cloaking belt even ZantCorp security couldn't crack to make him face the gate again, walk forward in dripping silence disturbed only by the occasional beep of one of the gate's biologic sensors or the whir of a robot gun turret. Now the chill, metallic air that hung around the gate enveloped him, weighing on him with its thousands of kilograms of cold. He took a trembling breath and climbed through a narrow maintenance hatch, holding in his hand the pistol he had taken from the ZantCorp guard.

Beyond was blackness that stank like rotten garbage and human offal. He edged forward, stopping every thirty seconds to listen and get his eyes used to the darkness. They didn't get used to it. The tunnel beyond the gate sloped gently downward. He stayed near the slimy, moss-covered right-hand wall, touching it every few meters. He wondered if Quasar was really there or if he was all alone in this darkness. At least there would be no Maggots or sewer tribespeople; Death Hole Warren was one of the few access shafts still used to send captured mutants to the underground land, and so was sealed off from the Boundary Zone and the sewers and tunnels above it where the tribes lived.

Then he saw a light. A very faint light far ahead in the darkness, that wavered and went out and came again. He crept toward it. Once or twice he thought he heard something behind him and turned around violently, but there was only darkness. He had walked perhaps two hundred meters when the light came on thirty meters ahead. He froze. Someone was shining a flashlight on four dark, cryptlike openings at the end of the tunnel, the openings of the shafts that went half a kilometer down into the earth, to where the mutants from the biowars lived in the shelter-city.

It was Quasar Zant.

She wasn't cloaked; the cloaking belt would have blocked her flashlight. Her self-destructive behavior was not manipulative but real, he now understood, watching her crouching by the openings in a cheap grey jumpsuit. Even though she thought there was no one to rescue her, she was going to go through with it, go down into the Warrens. She really wanted to die.

He opened his mouth to call her and there was a noise, but it didn't come from him. It was a heavy metallic scraping, like a manhole cover being dragged. Quasar took two steps backward and stood still, her flashlight on one of the openings. Karmade flattened himself against the tunnel wall.

People came out of the opening—at least they looked like people at first. Four of them fanned out around Quasar, staying a few meters away. One held what looked like an antiquated machine gun. Then a giant came out—a man or woman or something with no hair and very little face. Karmade didn't have time to look closely, because at that moment he saw something else. He *had* been followed in the tunnel. A pair of yellow eyes glinted in the glow from Quasar's flashlight, and around them a nonhuman shape bulked in the dark, snuffling at the mud where he had walked. The hair prickled on Karmade's head. He shrank against the tunnel wall, his gun in both shaking hands trained on the yellow-eyed thing, trying to watch both it and Quasar at the same time.

Another giant had come into the tunnel, and somebody in a ragged, hooded robe. The second giant was carrying something against its stomach, something spindly, white-haired, and helpless-looking. It seemed to have three arms with a few fingers on the end of each. The arms waved in slow, hypnotic arcs, and the thing mumbled as if doing magic spells. The giant carried it close to Quasar.

The spindly thing waved its three arms in front of her.

Then it hissed: "Someone watches." Everybody and everything in the tunnel looked in Karmade's direction.

Then one of the mutants who had fanned out around Quasar said, "It's just a slime-dog."

The spindly mutant craned around in the giant's arms as if to see, though Karmade could tell that it was blind, its eyes covered with pale skin.

"Go away, little brother," it hissed. "Run down your hole before the godies get you. Go away, little brother."

The yellow-eyed thing whined and snuffled at the mud three meters from Karmade, but as the mutant kept talking, commanding it, it turned around and its vague shape loped into the darkness.

Karmade leaned against the slimy wall breathing dizzily. When he could pay attention again Quasar was standing frozen, looking at the spindly, three-armed mutant.

It was waving its arms as if caressing an invisible bubble around her. It began nodding its withered head.

"Very soon." Its hisses echoed eerily in the tunnel.

"Very soon." Then it stopped waving its arms. "Come with me," it said to her.

"Tell me here," said Quasar, and her voice was sweet and clear in that dead place, though it trembled.

"Come with me," hissed the thing.

"Tell me here," said Quasar. "I don't want to go any farther."

"Come with me," hissed the thing, and motioned with a few of its fingers to the ones surrounding her. One of them stepped forward and grabbed her arm.

They didn't tell you in VR Safari that your hands would tremble so when it came to really shooting someone, but the targeter on the ZantCorp gun was good. Karmade tapped the trigger and the bloodied mutant spun away from her.

The mutant with the machine gun snapped around and poured metal down the tunnel, the hiss of his gun drowned out by the thud and shatter of bullets in the walls and mud around Karmade. Karmade tried to bury himself in the floor.

Silence suddenly echoed in his ears. He lifted his head. Smoke floated in the air. The mutants had gone. He stood up slowly, stumbled, then sprinted forward. There were two figures lying in the mud at the end of the tunnel. One was Quasar. Karmade knelt and ran his hands over her sobbing, violently trembling body. There was no blood, no hurt. He looked down at the mutant he had killed. It was a minor type, illegal but not a monstrosity. He turned back to Quasar, grabbed her arm.

"Let's get out of here," he rasped. Her wild, unconscious eyes looked right through him. He remembered he was cloaked.

He threw her over his shoulder and ran wildly up the tunnel toward the distant smudge of light that was the Warren-gate.

She seemed unconscious as Karmade carried her back to the 77th Sector flophouse. No one paid attention to them even though her cloaking belt was turned off. He

guessed that was because the Zant belts worked like
other cloaking devices, suspending a millimeter-thick
cloud of refractive dust around the cloaked object, a
computer keeping the orientation of the particles just
right to direct light around the object. So two objects in
close contact could be cloaked by one device, provided
its field was strong enough.

There was an incinerator chute in the flophouse hallway; Karmade laid Quasar on the dirty carpet and
stripped her, then stripped himself, and stuffed their
clothes—everything except the cloaking belts—into the
chute. If the authorities found out—even from circum-
stantial evidence like chemical analysis of mud traces—
that they had been in a Warren-tunnel, the best they
could hope for would be lengthy prison sentences.

In their room Karmade carried Quasar into the sanitary closet, sat her limp against the wall, and punched up
an expensive full-water shower. He soaped and sham-
pooed her all over twice, washing off every trace of
Warren-Hole mud, then did the same for himself. The
water seemed to slowly revive her; when he had finished
and had the airjets on she started dizzily trying to stand.

He helped her up and tousled her hair in the jets to
get it dry. It was black as nothingness, soft as silk, curl-
ing against her milk-white skin in patterns of exquisite
chaos. When it was dry and he let go of her he found she
was staring at him.

Her eyes were peculiar. He had never studied them
before. Black as her hair, like bottomless pits, up close
they made you dizzy, as if you were falling. He pulled
away from them with an effort, went to punch up the
room vendor's clothing menu.

There was a sound behind him, a cry.

He turned. Quasar was leaning against the sanitary
closet wall as if fainting again, sweat coming out on her
freshly dried body, gleaming in the flat lumtile light.

He took her arm. "Are you all right?" He was still
numb from the trip to the Warren-Hole.

Her eyes fluttered open and she looked at him from a

face suddenly changed, like someone else's face; as if, for the second time that night, a new person had entered her beautiful body.

She let out a gasp of breath like perfume. The nipples on her perfect breasts were erect. Her sweat smelled sweet; it made his head spin.

He laid her on the coarse, sagging bed.

Her heart beat in his body, pumping his blood. Her lungs made his chest rise and fall. He felt her cries in his throat. Their brains were tangled together.

Vaguely at the edge of his vision he imagined he saw something: an unblinking, winged Eye floating just above them, as if keeping watch over a fateful thing.

Afterward for a long time he watched her lie as if unconscious in her tumbled hair, the barest swell in the flat muscles of her belly showing she was breathing.

Finally he sighed, sat up dizzily, and started to scroll through the room vendor's clothing menu for something to wear. There was a hiss behind him.

Quasar's body arched on the bed in a convulsion so intense that her knotted muscles and swollen veins looked as if they would burst her skin, her face a hideous death mask. She shook helplessly, blood coming from between gritted teeth; then she collapsed, her crimson flush suddenly turning waxy grey, as if she were dead.

The hall door exploded and half a dozen ZantCorp soldiers burst into the room.

# 4

The place he got taken to, hands manacled behind his back and still naked, was on one of the innumerable floors of Sentrex. He rode down a huge white marble hall in a silent wheeled transport filled with ZantCorp soldiers. At the end of it was a place big enough to have weather, made all of white marble and enormous crystal chandeliers. As they rode across the endless floor the air above them seemed to thicken and get hazy, and a cloud formed.

The transport stopped and Karmade got hustled out by two soldiers. The marble was cold on his feet.

Shimmering on top of the cloud twenty meters above them was a huge throne of white marble with two smaller seats below it. A woman sat on the throne. She was slender and pale-skinned, with straight raven-black hair that fell to her shoulders. She was beautiful; in fact she looked a lot like Quasar Zant, whose aunt Karmade knew she was. But there was something frightening about the wideness of her black eyes, the tightness of her lips, the haughty intensity with which she held her head.

A man and a woman sat in the lower seats. The man was Thomas Rothe, Sentrex security chief. The woman was small, dumpy, nondescript.

The two soldiers hustled Karmade onto his knees and forced his head into a bowed position.

After a few minutes a woman's vastly amplified voice made him jump echoing in the huge space. Despite its loudness it was neutral, dull: "Mr. Karmade? Mr. Theodore Karmade?"

He looked up at the dumpy, nondescript woman who had talked, but one of the soldiers forced his head back down roughly.

"Yes," he muttered. His voice was flat and tiny.

"I am Dr. Ziller, Ms. Quasar Zant's personal psychoneurologist. I have just been informed that Ms. Zant has suffered an acute decompensation crisis as a result of your sexual assault on her. Because you yourself have received some psychoneurological training, I need not explain why a full and immediate description of this assault episode is indispensable to Ms. Zant's treatment."

Karmade stared at the white floor, fighting panic. "I didn't assault her."

"What *did* you do?"

"We had—we had consensual sexual relations."

"There is no such thing as consensual sexual relations with Ms. Zant," said Dr. Ziller patiently. "As you had a chance to observe, sex causes acute, highly destructive epileptoid seizures in her."

"But—we did. Ask her, and she'll—"

"Ms. Zant is frequently hallucinated and suffers from chronic, severe personality disorders, Mr. Karmade. She has been adjudged incompetent to manage her own affairs by the City Psychiatric Court. Her statements and judgments cannot be accepted as reality-based even under the best of circumstances."

"I didn't assault her."

"We waste time, Mr. Karmade. The only way you

may be able to repair some of the damage you have done is by quickly and truthfully describing everything you and Ms. Zant did from the time you abducted her in the Hak Lun pervodrome until ZantCorp security apprehended you."

He was ice-cold and sweating. The floor hurt his knees. He guessed he was being lie-detector monitored, so he tried not to even think about Death Hole Warren.

"I didn't abduct her. She insisted—"

"Mr. Karmade, let me clarify your situation, though it should require no clarification. Kidnapping and rape are capital offenses. Before turning you over to the City authorities for prosecution, Ms. Nelda Cloud, Ms. Zant's aunt and guardian whom you see here above you, has kindly agreed to let me interview you out of a concern for the well-being of her niece. If you cooperate completely and provide the information needed to structure Ms. Zant's treatment regimen, Ms. Cloud may be moved to request that the City authorities commute your death sentence to a prison term. However, absent such cooperation it is inevitable that Ms. Cloud's close connections in the City court system will take the same view of your case that we do, and impose the severest penalty. Do I make myself clear?"

A tiny light clicked on in Karmade's head. If they were monitoring his brain field they would see that, see the desperate guess at a wild theory as a P300 ERP on his trace, he realized a split second later. Maybe that was good. There was no choice now but to gamble.

He tried to keep his voice steady. "OK. I agree. Just turn me over to the City police and I'll tell them what I know." No one answered. He glanced upward and saw that the Ziller woman was studying a holo readout. His heart thundered as he went on desperately. "If kidnapping is a crime, so is malicious neglect of an incompetent. If Ms. Zant is 'disturbed,' maybe it's because she spent twenty hours on a hypothalamic transducer a few days ago."

"Do not think you can use your knowledge of Ms. Zant's problems to blackmail us, Mr. Karmade. In fact, your insolence is beginning to anger Ms. Cloud."

A boot hit Karmade, knocking him sprawling. He was suddenly painfully aware of his nakedness; he curled up on the floor protecting his genitals.

"Stop!" thundered the Ziller woman, her voice not dull anymore but full of something frightening.

The ZantCorp soldier froze in midkick.

"Anyone harming this man will be interviewed by Ms. Cloud personally," hissed Ziller. *"Personally."*

Fear suddenly filled the soldier's face, and he stepped backward. Karmade looked up himself, unnerved by the strangeness of the threat. Ziller's eyes were wide and her hand was raised as if she had uttered some awful curse. But even more terrible, Nelda Cloud's strange, wide eyes were fixed on him, on Karmade—and he imagined with revulsion that they were focused on the place between his legs.

The high-speed transvator they hustled Karmade into didn't stop and only slowed down for direction changes, but by the time they got to what looked like the Ziller woman's office she was already there, sitting behind a large, circular desk as if she had been for hours. The soldiers shoved him into the office but stayed outside, the door shutting on their jeering faces. He stood trembling on soft brown carpet, excruciatingly aware now of his nakedness, as if Nelda Cloud's eyes had torn some protective covering from him.

The office was hushed, circular, a quarter of its circumference floor-to-ceiling window showing an evening scene in the savannah of biocide-tolerant mutant prairie grass outside the City, its strange, deserted serenity a stark contrast to Karmade's panic.

Ziller's desk was neither tidy nor messy; it gave the same impression as the woman herself—of averageness, mundaneness. Ziller wore a plain, light blue suit that fit her poorly. Up close her short hair was grey, her eyes muddy brown, her face lined, patient, neutral.

"Mr. Karmade," she said, and her voice without amplification was even duller than before. "Come in. Sit down." She gestured to a chair in front of the desk.

Karmade sat down almost before he knew it. His nakedness had begun to unnerve him into submissiveness. It was an atavistic dominance-ranking phenomenon, he knew.

"I apologize for the unpleasantness in the audience chamber, Mr. Karmade. As much a show for Ms. Cloud's benefit as anything else. She is unfamiliar with the concept of cooperation among professionals. You are willing to help us with Ms. Zant, I presume."

Alternating confrontational and solicitous demeanors was a classic interrogation strategy, Karmade knew.

"I need some clothes," he said, his voice shaking despite his effort to control it.

Ziller looked at him thoughtfully for a minute, then flicked a little blue spot in the air. It turned red. "Bring Mr. Karmade some clothes."

In less than a minute a soldier stepped in with a handful of folded grey fabrics. He unlocked the manacles on Karmade's hands and helped him put on the clothes. They seemed slightly damp but otherwise comfortable.

When the soldier was gone and he was seated again, rubbing his wrists, Ziller repeated, "Will you help us, Mr. Karmade?"

He watched her fearfully, suspiciously. "I just want to get out of here," he said. Yet the clothes were helping him relax. He might get out of this in one piece, he realized. ZantCorp was said to be anxious to hush publicity about Quasar Zant, and turning him over to the City authorities would do just the opposite. Just keep acting innocent; there was no way they could suspect about the Warren. "It wasn't my fault. I'll do anything you want if you'll just let me go."

The woman nodded. "Good. We have been hearing about your—adventures from Ms. Zant, who has been talking under her medication, but I'd like your perspective. Please describe in detail everything that happened from the time you left Hak Lun's to the time you were found."

They couldn't prove anything from the ravings of a psychotic under medication, even if what Ziller said wasn't a bluff. Karmade tried to get his thoughts organized, then started talking slowly and hesitantly, warming up as he got going. The woman sat like a lump of clay, hands clasped on the desk, watching him. He assumed he was being lie-detector scanned, so he went into detail about how he had tried to stop Quasar from leaving the Dusk House, how she had tricked him, how he had gotten her into the flophouse to wait until ZantCorp security found them. He tried not to even think about the part he was leaving out as he passed over it, so that the ERP on his brain trace would look like a random fluctuation.

"I had no intention of having relations with her until she—made it difficult not to," he said earnestly and truthfully. "It was more than consent on her part, it was —you know?"

That was a nice touch; now he was on a lie-detector record telling the truth about not having kidnapped or raped Quasar Zant, and he would have the right at trial to demand that the record be produced in his defense.

"She initiated sexual relations with you?" asked Ziller carefully. Karmade studied her. He felt dizzy suddenly; the light in the office seemed to have concentrated around Ziller's face like one of those antique paintings where the subject is lit while the background is shaded in darkness. Her face seemed to sag like wet clay, the eyes slightly kindled with curiosity.

"Yes," he said, concentrating on making the word clear and definite. The dizziness was probably a stress reaction; at these close quarters there was no way an aerosol drug could be fed him without affecting Ziller too; and there had been no other means of administration.

She nodded gravely.

"Now tell it to me again," she said soothingly. "The whole story this time. What happened after you got the rental room?"

So they had picked up the ERP. He liked this woman, Karmade realized suddenly. She had him dead to rights, was no doubt being fed ongoing lie-detector and psychoneurological analyses through an earpiece, but she was being civilized about it, treating him like a fellow professional. She knew that what had happened could in no way be blamed on him. It would be a lot easier and less confusing to tell her the whole story. And the worse his dizziness got, the more he wanted to tell her, babble out everything, get it off his conscience so he could rest, go to sleep . . .

"Don't worry," the woman soothed him. "Ms. Zant is fond of you, Ted. She's been doing a lot of talking about you. It seems you're going to find something for her. What is that, Ted? What are you going to find for her?"

Something swam dully into Karmade's brain then, dim and vague.

The clothes. The clothes had been damp, still were damp, clinging to his body, probably soaked in cholineacetyltransferase and dopamine and methionine enkephalin or some other truth drug—

He stood up drunkenly and started desperately trying to pull them off. "God damn you," he said. He started to cry.

Dr. Ziller lifted a patient, neutral hand as if signaling to someone, and the lights went out.

·    ·    ·

There was a hospital bed on a beach, facing out across the ocean so that the person in it could breathe the fresh ocean breeze, be shaded from the hot sun by the great leaves of palm trees that rustled overhead.

The person in it was Quasar Zant, skin almost as pale as her white nightgown, scores of electrodes attached to her head.

Her eyes were closed, her face drawn and troubled as if with bad dreams, but as Karmade came near, obeying a direction he could not right now recall, they fluttered open and slowly focused. They were wide, innocent; despite the medical hardware, she looked like a child, many years younger than the desperate woman he had chased into the Warrens.

Color came into her skin as she saw him, a red flush. She started to gasp rhythmically, her chest heaving as if it was hard to breathe.

"Touch her," said a voice in Karmade's ear, a woman's patient, neutral voice. "Reach out and take her hand."

Karmade jumped, looking around. No one was there.

"Touch her," said the voice again. It had the flat, tinny quality of a pipe-in, and he didn't think the girl could hear it.

"We will treat her sexual phobia panic reaction by reciprocal inhibition," said Ziller's voice as Karmade still hesitated. "As soon as you touch her, reproducing the terrifying sexual stimulus, we will flood her central nervous system with endorphins and enkephalins, associating the stimulus with reward, thus systematically desensitizing her. Our use of your crime as an opportunity to treat her, and your cooperation with us, should mitigate your wrongdoing in Ms. Cloud's eyes. Now touch her."

All that made sense; it brought things back into focus, except for the last few hours—or was it few minutes? He had a hazy memory of an office—

He put his hand out toward Quasar. Her childlike eyes filled with terror and her gasping became uncontrolled, spasmodic. He pulled his hand back.

"Touch her," said the patient voice.

He put out his hand.

A centimeter before he touched her a bolt of lightning forked through his brain and body.

He screamed, dancing like an electrocuted marionette on the wires he suddenly realized held him up in the simulation room where Quasar lay, into which he had only imagined he had walked, while wires controlled his movements from somewhere above—he a nobody, an empty shell, moving and talking only as he was ordered by a god he couldn't see, but one who hated him.

But when he was done screaming and vomiting, the warm, sour liquid making a track down his chest, he was back again in the bright sunlight, standing over Quasar in her hospital bed.

"Mr. Karmade, I'm terribly sorry," said Ziller in his ear. "By mistake I forgot to turn off Ms. Zant's personal shield, which we have put in place because of her extremely sensitive condition. It gave you an aversive stimulus when you got too close. Do not be alarmed, the stimulus is harmless. I am turning off the mechanism now. Please let us try again. It is necessary to the treatment. I will be obliged to you if you will try again."

He was cursing, shaking so that he could not have stood up without the wires. He looked through his own pain into the pain in Quasar's eyes as he shakily reached for her again—

The bolt this time was much stronger than before, so strong that after a minute of confusion he seemed to be out of his body looking down, and he saw clearly that he was wired to a holo-cloaked machine mounted on the ceiling of the small simulation room and run by white-coated technicians—an aversive-conditioning rig. He re-

membered now being brought here from Ziller's office
and being given medication—

Then he was back on the beach flaming with the
long ebb of neuroelectrical pain and despair, his throat
sobbing in air to scream again, hands clawing wildly at
nothing.

"You see?" Ziller's voice was saying soothingly, not
privately anymore, and he knew it was talking to Quasar.
"He can't touch you. No one can. No one can ever
touch you. You see? Don't worry. No one can ever
touch you."

"Touch her again," the voice said privately to
Karmade. "One more time."

"No!" he shrieked.

"The stimulus won't hurt you permanently," Ziller
said patiently. "If you don't do it I'll administer it to you
right where you are, and I'll turn up the amplitude. Now
touch her.

"Or," she said when he just sobbed and shook, "you
can tell me what you and she did after you got the rental
room in the 77th Sector. Tell me that and I won't give
you the stimulus. Tell me now."

He couldn't tell, wouldn't tell.

"Touch her," said Ziller.

Quasar's eyes on his were now innocent and inquisi-
tive, as if he had sucked all the pain out of her. Crying
uncontrollably, he put out a cringing, wobbling hand.

Ziller had turned up the amplitude anyway. His
scream died in his own ears before his lungs and throat
stopped screaming. He went away. He wasn't Ted
Karmade anymore. He wasn't anybody. He had no consciousness, no being.

As he faded away he could hear the neutral, patient
voice saying soothingly to Quasar: "You see? He'll never
touch you again. It's all right. No one will ever touch
you . . ."

                    .
                    .
                    .

Touch her      ⋯  Ziller's voice in infinite
Touch her      regress, in a never-ending dream
Touch her      where pain and horror follow his
Touch her      touching hand, follows the voice,
Touch her      follows Quasar's face, follows the
   .           pain, follows his touching hand,
   .           follows the voice, follows Quasar's
   .           face, follows the pain, follows the
   .           touch, follows the voice, follows
               the face, follows pain, follows
               touch, follows voice, follows face,
               pain, touch, voice, face pain touch
               face pain touch fac

# 5

Karmade could feel the nerve damage as he floated up from the exhaustion of conditioning sleep; could feel the hangover from the hypnotic drugs, the psychoneurological scarring from the aversive stimulation, the horror of the nightmare that had gone on and on without waking, the simulated dream they had used to irreversibly connect in his unconscious the idea of touching Quasar Zant with the agony, horror, and despair of the conditioning machine.

He moved a little, burying his head in a pillow, but that brought hammering pain.

He opened gritty, sticky eyes.

He was in a white room with no furniture except the bed he lay on. The room was empty, silent, softly lit.

He noticed that he was wearing white pajamas. He slowly and stiffly sat up, nursing his throbbing head.

A door was ajar in the wall opposite him. Through it came a narrow bar of sunlight, a breath of fresh outdoor air, the tempting gurgle of water. After a few minutes he got up and limped over to it.

The place beyond was floored with uneven rock that had patches of green lichen growing on it. A few meters from the door the rock dipped down to form a deep, flowing pool with flowering vines at the edges trailing in the clear, slightly rippling water, which flowed over more rock and into another pool, and the whole landscape as far as he could see was rock and water and lush vegetation, a clear river between high rock cliffs, and above them intense blue sky, hot sun, and puffy white clouds, the air perfumed with such fleeting delicateness that he wondered momentarily if the orange flowers on the vines could be real.

Peeping out between the leaves and flowers at the edge of the first rock pool was the nozzle of a soap hose.

The place was a bathroom.

After a minute of bleary staring, Karmade stripped and waded into the pool. The water was one degree cooler than lukewarm, languid but at the same time stimulating. He knew most of it had to be incredibly realistic holography but he couldn't see where the landscaping ended and the light show began. The doorway he had come through was a narrow, irregular cave in a rough rock cliff with wild grasses growing from crags and cracks. It would have been incredibly, heart-stoppingly beautiful if it had not brought into Karmade's mind with overwhelming nostalgia the meter-square sanitary closet back at his apartment, which, though he had left it only thirty-six hours ago, seemed like a faraway paradise from which he had been banished, a place where there had been nothing to worry about except his next job, where he could take pills at night and sleep without fear of death or prison or torture—

Someone was standing near the door of the bathroom and watching him.

He jumped, heart pounding, stood frozen up to his waist in water, too afraid at first to recognize the long sour face, unruly white hair.

The man smiled a little sadly. "Jeez, Karmade, calm down. They gave it to you that bad, huh?"

"Rothe."

"How you feeling?"

"I want to get out of here. I'll do anything you want. Just let me out."

Rothe shook his head. "Too late for that now. Too bad you didn't stay with our memory block and take the money we gave you for getting the girl off the 'ducer. You did a nice job there, I'll say that. I admit I didn't expect you to come through, but the psych people said the brain wave similarity between you and her was out of this world—they searched practically every profile in the City before they ran that phony ad on you.

"Too bad it didn't end there. But no, you had to come back and kidnap and rape the girl."

"Rothe," Karmade said, lifting his hands, voice trembling. "I didn't kidnap or rape her. You must have me down saying that half a dozen times by now, along with a lie-detector trace."

Rothe studied him. "Our rigs say either you're telling the truth or you're a psycho who really believes his own lies. I've got nothing against you personally, but under the circumstances the psycho option is more likely."

"What do you—what do you mean?"

"That there's no way she could have consented to sex with you or anyone else. She's had aversive conditioning against sex—of an intensity that makes what Ziller gave you look like massage therapy."

Karmade stared at him, uncomprehending.

Rothe was grim, thin-lipped. "Her symptoms now are what you'd expect if the conditioning was somehow overridden—if, for example, she was forcibly raped. And there's no other way it could have happened; her conditioning is that strong."

"But—they don't give aversive conditioning for sex —it's illegal except for compulsive criminals—"

Rothe shook his head. "Believe me, she's had it. And that means you're guilty.

"There's only one other possibility, a remote one,

but one that would let you off the hook. Conditioned associations work in both directions. If the girl had an experience that gave her feelings of horror, pain, and fear of the same intensity as her aversive conditioning, Ziller says that could unblock her repressed sexual impulse, making her maybe very aggressive for a while. Once the horrifying experience wore off, the inhibition complex would come back, causing seizures—" He broke off, seeming to listen to something Karmade couldn't hear, then grinned wolfishly. "You just showed a significant ERP. Did what I said ring a bell?"

The experience in the Warren-Hole—

"Well, we—we watched a gossip column about her parents, and it got her very upset—" Karmade stuttered truthfully. A lie would show up on his brain trace and Rothe would hear about it through his earpiece in seconds.

Rothe shook his head. "The kind of experience I'm talking about would be a thousand times more powerful than that."

A realization came to Karmade despite his fear, and sudden rage washed over him, bubbling out of the black hole Ziller's conditioning had left in his brain. "What are you looking for, Rothe? The psych profile you ran to hire me would tell you I'm not the kind of hyperdopaminergic who could beat your lie detectors. So you *know* I didn't rape her. I guess it's just coincidence that you're here asking questions after that Ziller bitch electrocuted me." He shivered. "The nice, sympathetic security man who wants to help, and of course I gratefully tell you whatever you want to hear."

Rothe's grin was amused for all its sourness. "You're pretty tough, aren't you," he said softly. "Strange for a hack brain doc who can't even get a job. But there's another funny little ERP on your brain trace, just like last time. Comes up every time you say things like you just said."

"Random artifact."

"Doesn't look like it's canceling out from the reads

we have." His grin was dangerous. "I could break you if they gave me the order to interrogate you. Don't think I couldn't."

Karmade started to object again, but Rothe cut him off. "Skip it. I'm here to lay things out for you, give you the drill for the rest of your stay with us. Strange: you almost kill the girl and now she's attached to you. Says we're not to let you out of here or turn you over to the City prosecutor. Ziller says the brain wave coherence between the two of you has broken her ego boundary or something; she thinks it'll help if we go along with it. That's why we had to do the aversion conditioning—if you're going to be around the girl we can't have you assaulting her again." He sounded apologetic. "I just came around to make sure they weren't lying when they said they hadn't damaged you.

"But some rules apply. The most important is that you don't let the girl hurt herself. She's crazy, Karmade —really crazy—and part of her craziness is that she tries to hurt herself. My job is to make sure she doesn't succeed, but it's not easy. Sometimes she's able to evade our surveillance hardware; that's how she got on the 'ducer without us knowing about it, and we're presuming that's how she got out of the Hak Lun 'drome. We don't know the details; you can help us with that.

"The girl's unpredictable. The predictive psych models Ziller's people build of her don't work because she's an MPD."

Karmade stared. MPD—Multiple Personality Disorder. Suddenly the pieces of Quasar Zant's behavior started to fall into place; the sudden swings from infantile depressive to hypermanic delusive to sexual appetitive—it should all have been obvious, but he had had troubles of his own—

Rothe smiled his grim, thin-lipped smile. "You starting to understand? That happens when you do aversive conditioning on a child; and she was only four when her parents started doing it to her."

Karmade stared in sick horror. "Why?"

"It's not your business. What you need to know is that it's impossible to predict when any one of her personalities will be active. We keep her under surveillance every minute of the day, wherever she is, whatever she's doing, but you saw how that worked out at the 'drome. So we want you to help us. Humor her, do what she wants, but keep us informed. You help us and who knows"—he got the smile again—"maybe we can help you."

He turned to leave. "Oh, and Ms. Zant is done with her therapy session for this morning and wants to see you."

He stooped into the rock cave and Karmade was alone again at the edge of the river under the blue sky, with the perfumed breezes and bright sunlight. He picked up the soap hose and scrubbed himself quickly, his fear and nausea at the thought of Quasar Zant making the water feel cold. By the time he finished drying in the hot wind that blew from nowhere when he climbed out of the pool, and put on the expensive suit that had somehow come to be lying on a rock ledge near the door, he felt dizzy and sick.

Strangely, the cave door no longer opened on the white bedroom where he had woken up, but on a low, plain passageway. A discreetly glowing purple line floated in the passageway at knee height, leading out the end of it into a vague, vast landscape.

"Please follow the line," a soft, disembodied voice said in Karmade's ear.

He hesitated, then walked. The line erased itself as he passed along it. He realized that he was sweating. Quasar Zant. Face touch pain.

The purple line led him between two enormous marble pillars into a hall the size of a City boulevard. The frescoed ceiling three stories above was reflected in a mirrorlike marble floor, and the far end was lost in distance lit by a soft glow that came from nowhere. Priceless wooden tables and cabinets were spaced along the walls between portraits, potted plants, and trees, staircases running up to mezzanines. At intervals there were ponderous, two-story doors, all closed. The hall was empty and so still that the shuffle of Karmade's boots sounded loud.

After perhaps a kilometer one of the enormous doors was open, and the purple line turned and ran through it.

The room within was too big to see across even if the view hadn't been obscured by the trailing branches of white-flowering trees set in squares of dirt sunk into the marble floor. Holography of a mountain scene from Before filled the near wall with vertiginous depth, and the remote ceiling was indistinguishable from blue sky. The purple line ran among the trees and soon he came in sight of a large couch tucked cozily into a tree bower, with someone lying against its big, soft pillows. Karmade's gasping and the pounding of his heart got so intense that he felt he was going to faint.

He had seen her in rags crawling through filth, sooty and muddy, hair tangled and greasy with sweat. But the young woman on the sofa was clean and prettified, wearing white slippers and loose white lounging pajamas of some faintly shiny material, raven-black hair a cloud around her head, pale cheeks tinged with pink, a clean black choker around her neck. Even through the agony of his conditioned terror Karmade could feel her exquisiteness like a radiation of physical heat.

And he hated her. The sight of her made him want to vomit with the ashen hatred Ziller's conditioning had planted in him. But he was too afraid to do that, too afraid to do anything but stop three meters from her and stare.

Strangely, she seemed afraid too. Her eyes followed him with an anxiety that bordered on panic.

Her face worked itself into a smile.

"Hi, Ted," she rasped gaily. "Did you like the bathroom? I had them give you that suite. I thought it was—" Her giggle was grotesquely unnatural.

"No."

The smile faded too quickly to have been real and was replaced by hunted anxiety.

"You didn't like it?" she said faintly. "You didn't think it was—be—beautiful?"

"No," he said again.

Her hard-fought composure fell apart. She started to gasp. Her eyes, suddenly red-rimmed, were a mixture of panic, hate, and desperate self-control.

"Why did you touch me?" she screeched wildly. She gritted her teeth and he could see her master herself with enormous effort. "I can't let you touch me anymore," she rasped. "Don't you under—? There's something wrong with me, can't you see?" Her voice rose to a scream and she stood up, clenching white-knuckled fists.

Karmade staggered with fear. Only the pleading in her voice kept him from running.

"My parents—did something to me," she stuttered, a wild trembling choking her. Tears ran down her face, not from emotion, it seemed, but as a physical reaction to the violence of her self-control. "They—tore my mind. You understand?"

She looked sick, ashen. She sat back down and put her face in her hands dizzily.

"So we can't touch ever again," she whispered after a minute. "I'm—I'm sorry about what they had to do, but it's your own fault—"

"I don't want to touch you ever again," he rasped. "I want to get as far away from you as I can. I want to get out of here, go back to being—whatever it is I was." He rubbed his hand over his forehead distractedly.

"No," she said flatly, face still in her hands.

"Ask her why not," a patient, neutral voice said privately in Karmade's ear.

This time he fell down with terror, down on the floor with the conditioned panic Ziller's voice brought over him. Quasar lifted her head and looked at him in bleary surprise.

"Ask her why she wants you to stay here," repeated Ziller.

"Why—why do you want me to stay here?" Karmade whined.

Quasar looked at him a few seconds longer, then closed her eyes and settled back on her pillows.

In a minute she seemed to be asleep, face relaxed, breathing so softly Karmade couldn't see her chest move.

He noticed suddenly that he was off balance, as if something had pushed him as he knelt.

A prickling spread over his body. The light in the room took on a silver tinge. And suddenly there were two Quasars, one still lying on the couch, eyes closed, the other backing away from him apprehensively, a thick black cloaking belt fastened around the waist of her white lounging pajamas.

He felt something around his own waist. He was wearing a cloaking belt too—the same kind he had worn in the utility tunnels under the Hak Lun pervodrome, pliable as cloth, heavy as metal, studded with instrumentation lights.

The belts provided tactile as well as visual and audial cloaking, he remembered. He hadn't felt her put it on him because his nerves were numbed by some field it gave off.

Someone crouched close behind him. He scrambled away fearfully on his hands and knees.

It was him, Ted Karmade—a dense holographic image of him projected by a coin-sized module lying on the rug, which he hadn't seen until Quasar had fastened the cloaking belt around him. He looked over at the Quasar lying on the couch. An identical module lay next to her, projecting her.

The image of him coughed realistically and shifted to a sitting position on the rug, arms crossed and head down in a posture of despair and fatigue, and shut its eyes.

The real, cloaked Quasar said, "This won't take them in for long. We have to hurry.

"I want you to work for me."

Karmade stood up, staring at her, his hands clenched. The realization came over him that no one could see the two of them, that the surveillance devices watching every square meter of Sentrex were as blind to the cloaks Quasar's parents had left her as the Maggots and Warren-gate sensors had been. He started to sweat, muscles bunched, body full of flame. He could hurt her now, hammer his fists into her beautiful, tense face, her delicate breasts and stomach, stain the white of her pajamas with her blood for what she had done to him—

He took a step forward and his heart burst, his head exploded with pain, and conditioned terror shook him to his knees.

When he could look up again, through stinging sweat, Quasar was watching him with barely controlled panic, ready to run. But what she saw in his face made her slowly relax.

"I want you to work for me," she said. Her eyes were like black jewels, flat and depthless. When he didn't answer she went on: "You don't have any choice. If I tell them I don't want you here anymore—they won't just let you go."

"Work for you," Karmade repeated hoarsely.

"Yes," she said. "I want you to help me find my parents."

He stared at her, and then, weirdly, he started to laugh. He stood up shakily, convulsed with laughter he couldn't stop, leaned on the couch and laughed with all the hurt and anguish and fear in him, and when he saw on Quasar's face how his laughter hurt her, he laughed harder, until tears ran down his cheeks, until he could hardly stand, until his laughter took on a wild, insane sound, and then choked on its own bitterness.

"Your parents are *dead*," he spat at her.

She cringed as if he had hit her, face wild. "They're not dead," she hissed.

He tried to laugh again but his throat was full of ashes.

"My mother said good-bye to me before they left,

on the night of the lab explosion. You don't say good-bye to someone before you die in an accident." Her eyes were full of haunted pleading.

"A compensatory hallucination," he sneered.

She shook her head. "I know what's real and what's a hallucination."

"Sure you do. That's why you have to be tranqed silly after every meal. That's why you've got an army of psych doctors watching your every move twenty-four hours a—"

*"I know it was real!"* she screamed, her face suddenly insane.

He liked this game. "Maybe she *did* say good-bye. Maybe they were going on a trip the next day but they got blown up before they could leave."

She didn't say anything.

"Maybe you had a dream after they died and imagined it was real as part of your decompensation."

She shook her head, but her face was grey.

"You can have your people kill me if you want," Karmade said. "But you better face the fact, Ms. Zant, that you're all alone in this great, big, friendly building with your servants and your toys and a brainful of loose wires."

That night in Karmade's bedroom a skylight clicked on with an image—real or simulated, he couldn't tell—of the full moon. It hung in soft, deep blue like an enormous opal, splashing cool silver light on the floor and bed. Karmade lay curled in his blankets like a sewer tribesman hiding in his hole, alternately shivering with cold and slick with sweat, wave after wave of terror and nausea and insane rage washing out of the black hole Ziller's conditioning had burned into his brain. Murmuring voices that fit the rhythms of his heartbeat and breathing whispered inside him, saying things he couldn't quite hear but that filled him with sick despair. In his lucid moments he bitterly regretted his loss of control with Quasar Zant that afternoon, and listened fearfully for the footsteps of ZantCorp soldiers coming to dispose of him at her orders.

Exhaustion must have dragged him down into sleep because the next thing he knew he was sitting straight up in bed, heart pounding, trying to see what had woken him. The moon was gone from the skylight, replaced by tiny pinpricks in the blue-black sky. The room was empty: no Ziller come to torture him, no ZantCorp security personnel with a lethal injection, no Rothe with a list of questions.

He rubbed sweat out of his eyes, lay back down stretching tensely. Probably a nightmare, one of those that get you halfway out of bed before you wake up. He tried to relax on the soft pillow.

Something closed around his left wrist. He jerked it away with a terrified yell, nearly yanking his hand off as the thing cut into him. He rolled over and clawed at it with his other hand.

It was a handcuff. He was locked to the bed frame with a handcuff.

A prickling spread over him. Someone sat on the edge of the bed wearing a shiny black bodysuit.

Karmade scrambled into a huddled position, left arm extended by the cuff but legs curled up, right arm curled around his head. Now he saw the heavy cloaking belt around his own waist.

The person sitting on the bed was Quasar Zant, and she put out her hand.

He seemed to hear himself scream from a long way off.

The hand stopped. Her face was shadowed; he couldn't see her eyes.

"Don't you know it'll kill me," he managed to slobber. There was another Karmade stretched out like a peaceful spirit next to him, like his eternal, serene soul a million light-years from here, but projected by a little black module. "The conditioning'll kill me if we touch. And you too—you too—"

Her hand moved again, slowly. He could hear himself shriek trying to get away, yanking and rattling the cuff, but then her hands went swiftly to his torn wrist and she pulled him off balance with unexpected strength, slacking his arm so he was no longer hurting it. He sprawled on his side, feeling her hands like high-tension wires, gasping and sobbing but not dying.

After all, it was her touching *him*, not that other thing he couldn't think about, it was *her* touching *him* voluntarily, not the other; maybe it was all right as long as he lay perfectly still and didn't do anything, didn't think, didn't feel, had nothing to do with any of it—

He lay semiconscious, gasping. He didn't feel her gently stretch out his other arm and click a handcuff on it, and the same with his legs, so that he was cuffed spread-eagled on the bed, didn't feel her hands gently running through his sweat-soaked hair, down the bunched muscles of his shoulders and heaving chest—

Then she zipped down the front of her bodysuit and wrestled her perfect pale body out of it.

Karmade screamed and couldn't control himself. A roaring split his head, shards of vision, sound, and feeling cutting him to ribbons like shattered glass.

In one of the shards a naked woman straddled a body arching with bone-breaking convulsions, its lips frothing, eyes rolled up in a dead face.

In another her sweat-moist lips said, *"Don't be afraid."*

In another, a grinning death's-head Ziller was burning him.

In another the jewel-black eyes that glittered in Quasar's face slowly drained away his pain, filling him with a strange calmness and clarity—

When the eyes released him he was rolling with her through an ocean of sensation in a long, slow wave that was the intoxicating smell of her sweat, the wet, electric feel of her skin, the rasp of her breath, the white smudge of her face.

He was broken. He watched dully while she took him like a puppet, gasping with his lungs, her heart beating in his chest, her veins pounding in his sweating body. The part of his brain where Ziller's shrieking fear lived had burned up, blown out like an overloaded fuse, leaving him lobotomized, pithed.

When it was over she lay motionless, eyes closed, breathing in short gasps as if some upheaval was going on in her body. Now that her will was withdrawn from him he lay limp and helpless as a quadriplegic, unable to think or feel.

After a while she sat up and took off his cuffs, unbuckled his cloaking belt without even looking at his face, her movements mechanical, eyes blank as an android's. Then she and the holo of him disappeared as completely as if the whole thing had been a dream, leaving the room dark, silent, empty.

In a little while Karmade could move again, and his thoughts started to come untangled. Fear blared in him. What had just happened had to be the result of Quasar's multiple personality disorder, he realized. The pressure of sexual desire, strictly repressed because of her aversive conditioning, had manifested itself as an alternate personality the conditioned personality didn't know about. That alternate had emerged tonight, just as it had emerged in the 77th Sector flophouse. And if memories of its sexual activity "leaked" from the sexual alter to the conditioned personality—as they had last time—she would start her seizures again, and when that happened Karmade was done for. He couldn't stand up to any more of Ziller's aversion therapy, he knew. Or maybe they would turn him over to the City this time, or just kill him.

Why had the sexual alter chosen him for its acting out? Karmade wondered. There were plenty of other human and android males in Sentrex. Perhaps because of his unusual CNS waveform similarity with Quasar, which was the reason ZantCorp had hired him in the first place.

He thought feverishly as the night wore on, hoping whoever was monitoring his vital signs would think he had woken up with nightmares, a common occurrence after aversive conditioning. Should he make a break for it, try to escape from Sentrex? Security would catch him before he got halfway down the hall; and even if he did escape, the City offered no refuge from ZantCorp. Better to lie here and take the slim odds that the security people wouldn't guess about Quasar's supercloakers, that the medical people wouldn't see the evidence of intercourse, that the psych people would think the seizures were just a relapse.

# 6

After interminable hours of darkness the sun clicked on in the skylight. Karmade lay frozen, smelling Quasar's cold spoor in his covers. Minutes went by, a half hour without anything happening. Finally he got up, limped through the door to the holographic bathroom, and took a bath, barely noticing the cool water and perfume of the flowers. He was exhausted, sore, his left wrist raw and swollen.

He was drying off in the hot wind when he saw the purple line light up, leading out through the cave door. His heart hammered. Best to act innocent, as if nothing had happened. He put on the suit lying on the rock ledge and followed the line, emerging onto a staircase he couldn't place in relation to the giant hallway he had walked through yesterday. It was made of glassy pink stone, with a stone balustrade. It led down to a room whose floor, massive pillars, and ceiling were made of the same pink stone. The walls were glass, and outside them the bright upper reaches of sunlit air above the City blew by, shreds of brilliant cloud reflecting in the floor and pillars as they passed. The room was only thirty meters square with a five-meter ceiling: Karmade guessed it was in one of the narrow spires at the top of Sentrex. There was a pink couch in the middle of it and on that Quasar Zant was curled, wearing white slippers and a loose white gown that covered her chastely, watching TV.

He went toward her, relief filling him. She hadn't had a seizure. There had been no leakage between the sexual personality and the conditioned personality, at least not yet.

"—bury the seeds under two inches of earth," a voice was saying. A woman knelt on a holographic carpet of green, her hands finger-deep in dirt, a blond braid falling over her shoulder, belly swollen with pregnancy. "And water them once a day. This was how agriculture worked for thousands of years Before, and it was the basis of much of the food chain."

She was silent then, the only sound the strangely delicious rasp of her trowel in the dirt. It was Veronica Moen; Quasar was watching a public transmission from one of the L-5 satellite habitats that had been set up to conserve the pure genetic lines of human and other species until a decontaminated Earth—or some other planet —could be repopulated with them. Veronica was a second-generation L-5er, genetically perfect, beautiful, and strong, as all of them were in their pristine Class A environments. The live twenty-four-hour L-5 transmissions were encouraged viewing because they showed the wisdom of the government's program of maintaining genetic purity and patiently waiting until biocide levels on Earth had degraded to the point where the surface could be gradually reclaimed.

"The feel of the sun and fresh air, the smell of growing things, are *so* beautiful, *so* enlivening," murmured Veronica. "Everyone should have a chance to experience them, and I am confident everyone will."

That was a laugh. Government PR gave reclamation

start dates between fifteen and twenty years away, but it was rumored that the real figures were five times that.

It took a few minutes before Karmade realized that the sweating, pounding of his heart, and tightening in his chest at Quasar's proximity were less than yesterday. What had happened last night had undermined his aversive conditioning, he realized with a lifting feeling. After all, the conditioning was in effect just an artificially induced phobia, and one of the oldest methods for curing phobias was flooding—forced exposure to the terrifying stimulus.

A familiar prickling crept over him and a second Quasar was backing away from him, and he was wearing a cloaking belt.

Looking at the real Quasar some of his relief evaporated. Her face was drawn and troubled, forehead wrinkled, eyes haunted. Something was obviously wrong. Maybe there had been some interpersonality leakage after all.

"We have to go somewhere," she told him, scanning his eyes as if to decide if she could trust him.

"Oh, no. No more escapes. I told Rothe I'd let him know if you started planning something dangerous, and I will."

The Quasar replica shifted its position on the couch, watching the TV dully. A replica of Karmade stood nearby with tense weariness.

"—we have the right and every reason to survive—" Veronica Moen was saying.

"Are you a spy for Rothe now?" Quasar snarled, eyes red-rimmed with worry. "What have you told him? Anything about—the place we went? They're trying to get evidence on me, don't you understand? Anything they can. If my aunt could put me away permanently, all my money would be hers." Her wild eyes searched his face again, but the fear she saw there seemed to reassure her. She went on in a more confident tone. "*I* saved you from them, you understand? Why do you think they're keeping you alive? My aunt would have you compacted with the garbage like that." She snapped her fingers in his face. "*I* saved you—to work for me—so you better do what I say. If I find out you've been reporting anything to Rothe—*anything*—I'll tell them to get rid of you. Do you understand?"

"What kind of work am I supposed to be doing for you?"

"Helping me find my parents."

"Your parents are dead, Ms. Zant."

"Fine. Believe that if you want to," she said as if she had practiced the words, controlling her voice with difficulty. "It doesn't matter what you believe as long as you do what I say."

Suddenly her eyelids fluttered, her pale alabaster face flushed and broke into a sweat. She swayed on her feet.

But the fit seemed to pass almost at once.

"Are you all right?" he asked anxiously.

"Of course. What do you mean?"

She reached out quickly and touched something on his cloaking belt. Everything went pitch-black.

Without anything to see he felt dizzy, staggered trying to keep his balance. A small hand steadied him.

"Walk," said Quasar in his ear.

They began to walk. The droning of the TV faded. Karmade stumbled on the stairs. She helped him climb.

It seemed like a long way—longer than the climb down from his room—and at the top the space around him felt vast. Karmade imagined they were in one of the enormous halls, but it was impossible to tell.

After more walking Karmade got turned to the left. Something clicked in front of him. Quasar pushed him through a narrow doorway that hushed shut behind them, and he bumped into a wall. The air was motionless, stale. The floor suddenly dropped under him like a 'vator. When it stopped and they got out and Quasar touched his belt again, he blinked and squinted in the light of a plain, windowless room three meters wide and five long, in the center of which was a machine.

It had a massive black console and a padded table

with wrist and ankle cuffs. When Quasar flicked a switch on the console the light in the room dimmed and an enormous holographic control/annunciator panel rose into the air, numbers and symbols flickering with internal hardware and software checks. A helmetlike cylinder at the end of the table nearest the console came to life with a hum and crackle of ionization.

"You know what this is," Quasar said, watching him closely. "Turn off your belt. This whole room is super-cloaked, so we don't need them."

He fumbled with the thumbplates until the belt melted out of his hands and she disappeared. A moment later she reappeared without her own belt.

She took off her white slippers, put her hands behind her neck, and unclasped her black choker. Underneath on both sides of her neck were ugly blemishes in her perfect skin, like two plastic navels. Chronic silastic catheters embedded over her carotid arteries.

Karmade stared. An operation like that required a special exemption from the Mutant Control Act, of a kind given only in cases of severe mental disorder requiring massive drug doses directly to the brain. If she was that sick she was going to be hard to handle without the remote-operated drug necklace.

Quickly and gracefully she lay on the table, gown rustling, and squirmed into a comfortable position with her head under the helmet device, which Karmade had already figured out was a nuclear magnetic resonance imaging sensor, a machine for reading brain processes.

"You know how to work one of these, don't you?" she asked through gaps in the helmet's instrumentation. "I want you to—you know—fix me. My mental problems."

He stared at her, the richest person in the world, who had escaped from the City's most feared security force and defied a mutant kidnapping squad, yet whose naiveté was even more frightening than her strange abilities.

He could have told her that a tech-grade psych operator knew how to work a Central Nervous System Homeostatic Equilibration Device—or CNS-HED—like a subway train driver knew how to fly an interplanetary exploration platform. But he didn't. As long as she thought he could work it maybe she would go on thinking he was useful, wouldn't tell her Aunt Nelda to get rid of him.

"Fix you how?" he asked instead after a minute of careful thought. "What's the objective?"

She studied him through the helmet. "I know there are things I should remember, things I should be able to figure out but can't. They give me drugs that make my mind dead, and that *bitch's* 'directive subliminal therapy,' she calls it, that really just keeps me crazy so my aunt can go on controlling my money."

Paranoid delusions.

"There are things inside me, deep in some part of my mind that they want to keep me away from—I hear voices sometimes, telling me things—about my parents —that's crazy, I know"—probably leakage of alternate personality contents projected as voices—"but the information I get *is real*. If I could *just remember*, maybe I would know where my parents are, or figure out how to find them, get them to come back and get rid of my aunt, put me back together so that I'm like a human being . . ."

Looking down at her a strange emotion pierced the armor of fear, hate, and calculation that had become second nature to Karmade already in his few days at Sentrex. Pity.

"Tell me again why you think your parents are alive," he said.

"You don't have to believe they're alive, Karmade. You just have to—"

"Tell me." And when she was silent: "I won't laugh this time."

"Then listen to me, you bastard, instead of to your own voice." She got control of herself with an effort. *"They said good-bye to me.*

"It was at night. I was sleeping and my mother woke me up. There was a light from the hall and my mother was sitting on the edge of my bed, stroking my hair. My father was in the room too, telling her to hurry. I didn't know what he was talking about; he said, 'Hurry, Nova, it's starting—we don't have much time.' She just stroked my hair and whispered, 'Good-bye, little one. Good-bye. Daddy and I have to go now, but we love you, we'll always love you.' And then somehow I fell asleep again, and the next day they were gone and nobody would tell me where, and a few days later my aunt told me they were dead, and we went to a funeral, and everybody said they were in the coffins but we couldn't see them."

"Is that all?"

"Isn't that enough?" She was crying.

"You were a little girl," he said as gently as he could. She didn't seem decompensated, and the grief reaction was healthy. "You could have dreamed it and remembered it as real, or wished so hard for it to be real that you started to believe it. That happens. Everyone else believes they died in a laboratory explosion."

"That's not true."

"Somebody believes they're alive? Who?"

She shivered suddenly, clasping her arms around herself.

"That little man or person or whatever he was I saw —down there, he knows something about my parents," she whispered after a minute. "He says they're not dead. *He says he knows where they are.* His voice comes in my mind. He—he told me things about my parents, things nobody could know. He told me to meet him—down there, where you followed me—"

She looked up at him staring at her. "How do you explain that he came to meet me when I went down there? If I'm crazy, how do you explain that?"

"They may have heard you in the tunnel and come up to grab you."

"Didn't you hear how he talked to me? He *knew* me."

Karmade took a deep breath. Wondering at his own reasons for doing it when all he wanted was to get out of here, escape, he tried again. "Quasar, let's think about this, to see if what you believe makes sense. Even if your parents could have faked two corpses that genetic tests said were them, and slipped away into hiding, why would they do that? They were the richest people in the City. There was no trouble they couldn't buy their way out of. And if they did go, why not take their eight-year-old daughter? Can you think of any way that makes sense? And even if they *were* alive and hiding out somewhere, why would they tell some blind, three-armed mutant?"

"But that mutant knew I was coming to the Warren-Hole, didn't he?"

"Maybe. I'm not ready to discount the possibility that the voices you've heard are real. Nobody knows what the mutants have been doing down there over the years, or how they've evolved, but there's been talk of ESP development—telepathy, clairvoyance, that kind of stuff. Now, those mutants looked to me like they were trying to grab you, not talk to you. If you were a mutant and you could read people's minds, and you knew someone on the surface—someone rich—was desperate to find her parents, you might try to get your hands on her. After all, they hate us for making them live in those stinking holes and feeding them our garbage. You might send her telepathic messages—"

Her face was preoccupied, eyes withdrawn. He wasn't getting through to her.

"And even if they were alive," he ventured, "you might not want to find them."

That got her attention. "What do you mean?"

"Remember how I said they were rich enough to buy themselves out of any jam? Well, maybe there's an exception.

"What's the most serious crime in the City? What is it that schoolchildren are taught to hate, that people get so hysterical about that no amount of money could make it OK? That the security forces have orders to shoot on sight?"

When she just stared, he muttered the answer himself. "Mutants."

She came up from under the scanner helmet, face convulsed with rage. He warded off her fist. "My parents aren't mutants," she hissed, crouching now on the table. "They were colonization astronauts. They got more genetic screening than anyone in the City."

"Maybe they got mixed up with mutants somehow, or caught a mutagenic virus—"

"They wouldn't get mixed up with mutants. They would *never*—"

"Even the ones that tried to grab you in Death Hole Warren?"

She lunged at him, screaming to block his voice out of her head.

He held her struggling wrists, heard the crack of her teeth grinding.

Then suddenly she was still.

Her voice was distant, dreamy. "It doesn't matter. I'll go back there myself, into the Warren-Hole. I'll find a way, eventually, after they kill you. They can't stop me forever."

The CNS-HED was a device for treating chronic mental disorders by modifying the brain's homeostatic neuroelectrical/neurochemical equilibria, Karmade knew that much. New homeostatic balances were created using the brain's own chemicals, created so gently and subtly that, in theory, the brain afterward maintained the new balances naturally. Invented by Nova Zant, it had been briefly celebrated before Mutant Control Act regulations made the surgical modifications needed for patient interface with the machine illegal. And anyway, in a society where most of the population had been psychologically damaged by humanity's traumatic recent history and the loss of the ecosystem, the expensive, time-consuming approach of the CNS-HED was ill-suited to the desperate need to keep as many people as possible functioning at the least cost.

Karmade sat on a dusty swivel chair in front of the 'HED's enormous holographic menu array and tried to figure out a way to use the machine to convince the woman on the table that she should keep him alive.

He had knocked her out as soon as the NMR helmet's catheter attachments had clicked into the plugs in her neck, flicking his fingers through the Induction menu entries for Stage 1 Sleep/Non-REM and Neuromuscular Blockade. He guessed he didn't have long to figure something out; eventually someone would try to talk to the two holographic dummies back in the pink marble room.

The menus hanging in the air were in three main blocks: Somatic, Neurochemistry, and Electroneural, each divided into CNS and Peripheral categories, with long submenus. The readouts specified two different modes of operation: Instrumentation, in which the machine measured the subject's physical and psychoneurological parameters, and Reequilibration, in which the machine fed neurochemicals, precursors, antagonists, reuptake inhibitors, and the like to the subject's brain through the catheters in her neck.

Karmade hesitantly flicked a finger through the Somatic Instrumentation submenu for Peripheral Circulatory System Status, just to get an idea of how the machine worked. Further submenus, for Cardiogram, Respiration Rate, Alveolar Gas Exchange, Serum Chemistry, Blood Count, Vascular Pressure, and many other parameters unfolded. He flicked a finger through Serum Chemistry and got a further display of about a hundred blood chemicals, their concentrations fluctuating slightly even as he watched, cycling in gentle rhythms he could almost feel, the pulsating dance of Quasar's life, hypnotic as the ebb and flow of the sea.

He had an idea.

With a sweating hand he switched the Serum Chemistry display to Reequilibration mode. The readouts

changed to Reequilibration submenus. He found the
submenu for the chemical vasopressin, flicked it, and
found himself facing a large, intimidating panel. He
studied it. It contained options for perturbing blood serum vasopressin in dozens of ways.

He shakily selected Episodic Mode, Single Episode,
100 mg. Vasopressin was a relatively innocuous circulat-
ing neuroactive peptide responsible for maintaining
blood pressure, certain kinds of memory retrieval, and a
few other things, but a shot of it should make Quasar
feel different when she woke up, as if he had run a treatment on her.

A panel leapt out of the submenu:

Subject:   QUASAR ZANT
Regime:   SINGLE EPISODE VASOPRESSIN
    100 mg
Monitoring Mode:   DEFAULT/GLOBAL
Last Procedure:   12/17/37
Operator:   NOVA ZANT
Begin Sequence?   [Y]   [N]

12/17/37. Quasar's last treatment on the CNS-
HED had been twelve years ago, with her mother, the
inventor of the machine, running it.

That would have been when she was eight years old,
shortly before her parents died. But why would they
have been doing 'HED therapy on their eight-year-old
daughter? And why in a supercloaked room?

Karmade stared at the display, thinking. Finally he
flicked the [Y] panel.

The machine gave a faint click and the bank of
menus vanished, replaced by a vast array of readouts,
data windows, brain maps showing blood flow and
neurotransmitter activity, and other graphs, diagrams,
and charts. One was a shimmering 3-D topographical
image of what looked like a mountain range woven from
colored threads. It depicted six valleys of varying depths
separated by plateaus and peaks. Karmade guessed from

the axis captions that it was a phase space map of
Quasar's neuroelectrochemistry, the valleys denoting at-
tractors or energy troughs corresponding to stable brain
states. If that was true, the graph showed that Quasar
had six personalities. He thought he had seen at least
three of them: one passive, infantile, depressive; one desperate, resourceful, strong; one mute, dissociated, sexual.

There was a tone, and an entry in a list of serum
chemicals was highlighted—it was the entry for Serum
Angiotensinogen, the vasopressin precursor normally secreted by the kidneys in response to low blood pressure
and converted to vasopressin by an enzyme in the lungs.
The 'HED was doing its best to mimic the natural production of the neurochemical by feeding Quasar the precursor through her neck catheters. A few seconds later
the entry for Angiotensinogen Converting Enzyme in
the lungs showed a drop as it was taken up by the angiotensinogen, and almost immediately the entry for Serum Vasopressin showed the level rising.

The Vascular Pressure display now began to show an
increase as the new vasopressin molecules docked in re-
ceptor sites in the neurons enervating the arteriole muscles sheathing Quasar's blood vessels, stimulating them
to tighten. CNS entries lit up showing increased vasopressin levels as the doped blood reached the brain. The
sleeping Quasar took a deep breath.

Then changes cascaded through the displays too fast
to follow as the second and third and fourth order effects of the vasopressin rippled through her: increase in
body temperature as capillaries near the skin contracted,
keeping blood heat in, triggering the hypothalamus to
mobilize vasodilation and sweating responses; increased
blood pressure stretching the afferent arterial vessels of
the kidneys, stimulating the juxtaglomerular cells to reduce their secretion of angiotensinogen; the atrial chambers of the heart also detecting the increase in pressure
and secreting atriopeptin to signal the kidneys to divert
more fluid to reduce blood volume. Quasar's homeo-

static feedback loops were returning her blood pressure and other disturbed parameters to their normal resting states. Karmade watched rivulets of yellow, gold, green, violet—vasopressin and the other chemicals secreted in response to it—flowing into and across the topographical map of her brain neuroelectrochemistry, subtly altering it, eroding here, silting there, changing the shape of a feature there, filling two of the troughs ever so slowly, inching them closer together, dissolving the watershed between them.

More minutes passed and sweat began to prickle on Karmade. The changes coming through the displays didn't seem to be slowing down. Quasar's neurophysiology wasn't settling back into an approximation of its previous state as it was supposed to. Instead, somehow, a number of neurotransmitters seemed to be shifting their balances and taking important CNS neural activation patterns along with them. Acetylcholine, oxytocin, and prolactin spiking, GABA and dopamine dropping, especially in the reticular formation, 5-HT and epinephrine ramping up steadily, electrical activation and blood flow increasing in the post-central regions and decreasing in the frontal areas of the brain.

He glanced down at Quasar and fear shot through him. She was covered with sweat, her breathing rapid and shallow.

What had happened? How had a gentle nudge to a blood-pressure and memory hormone done this? Fighting panic, he tried to think. Maybe the vasopressin had knocked her from one personality to another—her sexual personality, probably, judging from the sky-high levels of oxytocin and prolactin. How it could have happened he didn't know, though perhaps a neurochemical that affected memory could change the expressed personality by changing the complex of accessible knowledge.

Whatever the cause, if Quasar Zant woke up a different person than she had been an hour ago, there would be hell to pay.

But he didn't know how to reverse the process.

There was a Help menu at the bottom of the holo panel. He flicked it, scrolling at top speed through submenu after submenu like a man lost in an endless house, sometimes coming back to a room he recognized but never understanding the overall plan. Finally he stumbled across HISTORICAL FILE.

He was desperate now, ready to grasp at straws. A picture of Quasar's past treatments might help him figure out what was happening to her and what to do about it.

HISTORY DEPTH?
Full.
HISTORY DETAIL?
Summary.

Record 1::1/21/33::Operator N. Zant::Subject Q. Zant::Age 48.0 mnths::Sex Female::Somatic Status Stable/Excellent:: Dwuwer Psychoneurological Status Inventory 24 Stable/Very Good::Procedure Pulsed Staggered High-Low Driving of Serotonin Dopamine Norepinephrine GABA Acetylcholine::

Karmade stared at the entry recording a 'HED procedure done on Quasar sixteen years before. Pulsed, staggered neurotransmitter perturbations were known to be pathogenic. He had never heard of them being used therapeutically—especially on someone rated "very good" on the Dwuwer scale—especially using the five most important CNS neurotransmitters, alternately driving them up and down.

Neurochemical Outcome Neurohomeostatic Crisis Eventual Reequilibration::Somatic Outcome Nausea Vocalization Perspiration Parasympathetic Mobilization Involuntary Muscle Contractions::Operator Notes None.

If he understood that, Nova Zant had given her healthy four-year-old daughter powerfully disequilibriating doses of critical neurochemicals, driving their concentrations in her brain separately first up and then down, causing vomiting, crying, and seizures.

He flicked the second record.

Record 2::2/3/33::Operator N. Zant::Subject Q. Zant::Age 48.5 mnths::Sex Female::Somatic Status Stable/Excellent:: Dwuwer Psychoneurological Status Inventory 20 Stable/Good::Procedure Pulsed Staggered High-Low Driving of Serotonin Dopamine Norepinephrine GABA Acetylcholine:: Neurochemical Outcome Neurohomeostatic Crisis **Partial Reequilibration Failure—Cycling Mode**::Somatic Outcome Nausea Vocalization Perspiration Parasympathetic Mobilization Involuntary Muscle Contractions Unconsciousness::Operator Notes None.

Karmade felt sick suddenly, his sweat turning cold. A healthy four-year-old child driven by this machine to screaming, vomiting, seizures, and finally unconsciousness—

Record 3::2/4/33::Operator N. Zant::Subject Q. Zant::Age 49 mnths::Sex Female::Somatic Status Unstable/Fair:: Dwuwer Psychoneurological Status Inventory 7 Cycling/Poor::Procedure Alternate Bipolar Equilibriation Driving of Serotonin Dopamine Norepinephrine GABA Acetylcholine:: Neurochemical Outcome Neurohomeostatic Crisis Partial Bipolar Reequilibration::Somatic Outcome Nausea Vocalization Perspiration Parasympathetic Mobilization Involuntary Muscle Contractions Unconsciousness::Operator Notes None.

Rothe thought the "sessions" had been aversive conditioning. That would have been bad enough, but here were records showing that her mother had purposely split Quasar's personality, first disrupting her brain's healthy neurochemical equilibrium, then driving the resulting chaotic neurochemistry to reequilibriate in separate energy troughs.

Karmade skimmed through a few dozen more records. There was no doubt about the purpose of the procedures but he was soon out of his depth as to the details. Nova Zant's expertise amazed him. The speed and skill with which she had destroyed and rebuilt her daughter's neurochemistry was staggering. She had worked systematically, aiming not for random splitting but obviously striving to dissociate Quasar's mind in specific ways. And then he came to an Operator Notes field in one of the records that had been filled in, the only one like it that he had seen. It was in Record 31, dated 4/4/ 35, when Quasar was six years old.

::Operator Notes My god. Irneldo will be angry if he learns I have written this, but I have to tell someone, even this demonic machine; I cannot endure it alone any more. No one knows the agony of a mother who tortures her baby, even though she knows it is for her own good, even though she knows it must be done. But her screams seems to tear the flesh from my bones, and her vomit is like my blood pouring from her mouth, sour and corrupt. And worst of all, when she is well and she comes to me shyly, and she cannot remember a thing that we did yesterday or even *her name*. Then a part of me dies, even though I tell myself that it would be worse if It had no room to grow in her, if It tore her to pieces awakening, that she is the most fortunate of children, that some day we will put her back together whole, better than whole, and we will all be back together some day

Quasar, soaked in sweat that plastered her dress to her and made her hair like liquid pitch, sighed and shivered in her artificial sleep. Then something strange happened.

A feature was beginning to form at the edge of the topographical map of her brain state, a small trough that looked like a quivering by-product of the neuroelectrochemical changes portrayed by the flows and dryings-up, the brightenings and darkenings of the multicolored threads that were the warp and woof of the diagram. As Karmade watched, the feature began to get bigger, first slowly and shakily, then more quickly.

It began to move. It flowed like a wave slowly toward the center of the diagram, deepening and sharpening as it went, until it was a dark slash rolling toward the personality troughs.

An alarm sounded and displays began to flash in all parts of the air. Life-Threatening Epileptoid Episode, one of them said. Numbers reeled as the machine automatically poured chemicals into Quasar, racing to reverse the rift in the map, that was now a yawning hole big enough to swallow all the personality troughs at once.

As it passed through the middle of the diagram, the personality troughs disappearing into it, two things happened.

A door seemed to open in Karmade's mind, a door he suddenly realized had been there all the time but that he had never used, and through it came—something—a feeling or perception. A sudden sense of freedom, along with an unshakable clarity amid the blare of alarms and flashing lights. It was as if he had been set suddenly atop a mountain even higher than Sentrex, so far above the City that nothing could harm him, and he looked down upon everything—

Simultaneously, Quasar opened her eyes—not sleepily or drugged, but all at once and with complete alertness, staring up through the gaps in the helmet—

And looking into her eyes Karmade saw the Eye: single, black, embedded in pink flame.

Then it was over. The door in his mind slammed

shut and he gaped again with fear at the neuroto-
pographical map; but by now the sinister gorge had slid
across it and off the edge, leaving its features wobbling
but intact. The alarm went silent; the flashing displays
went dark one by one.

Emergency Abort flashed and other readouts showed
the machine withdrawing its chemical tendrils from
Quasar. In a few minutes the catheters clicked out of her
neck.

7

Karmade wasn't sure what Quasar remembered when she woke up. She seemed disoriented, and kept asking what time it was. She lowered herself off the 'HED table and stood shakily, hair matted and clothes wrinkled with drying sweat. She turned his cloaking belt on but forgot to activate the function that blanked out his vision.

Part of one wall slid aside for them and a meter-square 'vator took them up a short way. It opened again and they stepped out into a giant hall like the one Karmade had walked through before, cabinets, portraits, and small tables holding vases of flowers spaced along the walls. The 'vator door sliding shut behind them was a full-length portrait of Nova and Irneldo Zant, both dressed in black, the vague outlines of their bodies shaded in darkness almost suggesting a serpentine inter-twining, their pale, nearly identical faces looking out of the canvas calmly. Karmade guessed you could only see the portrait door opening if you were wearing one of the supercloaker belts.

The pink marble staircase opened through a nearby

archway. Back in the pink room the holographic replicas sat at opposite ends of the couch staring dully at a show about an experimental teleoperated farm the government had set up in the biocide-resistant savannah a few miles outside the City. The transparent plastic shelter that protected the farm from the poisonous air and rain billowed in the wind next to a hill of tailings left after soil decontamination machines had processed the dirt inside.

". . . natural soil is now not far from the point where crops may be grown in it without fear of biocide poisoning," the scientific-sounding announcer was saying. "Already, stabilized mutant savannah grasses thrive in this marshy . . ."

Quasar hurried to the couch and sat on top of her replica, which casually moved to match her pose and vanished. Karmade followed more slowly.

After Quasar left the pink room without a seizure or other disaster, Karmade's fear slowly ebbed and was replaced by a surge of nervous energy. He spent the afternoon wandering, at first tentatively, and then with growing boldness, through the halls, rooms, staircases, passages, archways, gardens, and mezzanines of the giant building, turning his predicament over in his mind, trying to estimate his chances of escape and decide what he should do next, wondering whether his bungled session with Quasar on the CNS-HED would cause a personality reintegration crisis, and if so, what would happen. Despite his preoccupation, it came to him vaguely that he was a different person now than he had been three days ago when he had arrived at Sentrex. Sentrex had stripped away layers of illusion and fantasy, layers of superficiality, had concentrated his mind and made him one-pointed as only someone unshakably sure of his purpose in life can be. And his purpose was to survive.

No one tried to stop him from wandering through the building; he didn't even see anyone, though he assumed he was being monitored. He walked through huge halls whose floors of patterned crimson, emerald, and pink marble reflected the arabesques painted on vast ceilings and the gleam of fountainlike chandeliers sunlit through lofty windows. It was rumored that Sentrex contained parts of ancient palaces recovered from the moldering exoCity, carefully decontaminated and reconstructed. Giant doors opened into terraced gardens with what appeared to be *real* birds and buzzing insects, their blue skies and trees, clouds and fragrant breezes, making him want to sit forever in their hidden bowers and gaze out over their distant hills. At the edge of one of these gardens, in a courtyard of flower beds and palms where fountains murmured, trellises and bushes making nooks of shady privacy, slender alabaster columns held a delicately carved stone arch above an ornate door.

Beyond that door straining giants in white marble held the massive vaults of a low-arched grotto, a few candelabra on the walls throwing dramatic shadows along their beards and muscles. Karmade's feet tapped warily on the grey marble floor. Beyond the last vault was a broad marble staircase whose carved banister supported black iron lanterns. At the top of that was a hallway.

It was five meters wide and dark; Karmade could see only a little way down it. It was floored with polished stone, and along the right-hand side two-story arched windows separated by statues gave a faint starlight, which had to be simulated since by Karmade's calculation it was the middle of the afternoon. The left-hand wall was dark, murky, ominous.

Karmade stepped into the hall. Shapes leapt at him from the left-hand wall.

It was a depth-mural, he realized after his first fright, of the type the guilds and great familycorps commissioned to celebrate their accomplishments and lineages, and which unfolded as you walked along them, changing perspectives and scenes. He remembered that Irneldo Zant was supposed to have been an accomplished depthpainter.

The shapes that had leapt at him with their drawn, dirty faces, their thin, ragged-clothed bodies straining to lift or pull something, stayed motionless until he moved again, and then, as he walked slowly into the hall, they merged into a mass of other struggling shapes under a dark, poisoned sky. After a few steps he realized that the mural depicted the years of the Consolidation, the turbulent period when Nova Cloud and Irneldo Zant had been children and when it had still seemed possible that the human race would perish in the aftermath of the biowars. As he moved down it, Karmade saw portrayed the collapse of the two other Earth cities that had survived the wars, their inhabitants dying of biocide poisoning, disease, and hunger; the mass biocide poisonings in this last City as makeshift, overburdened decontamination systems failed; famine taking almost half the City's population; the food riots; the suicide construction teams laboring to build shelter from the poisoned air, water, and earth. Here Karmade thought the figures of Irneldo and Nova gleamed out in the shifting kaleidoscope of images: a little boy working alongside his parents in the prototien factories; a beggar girl with haunting eyes huddled on a half-demolished street. A little farther on coats of arms shone out of the turbulence, the heralds of the great families and guilds that had coalesced into the neofeudal social structure that had pulled the City through the Consolidation and brought the human race to its present prospects of almost certain survival, each family and guild decontaminating, rebuilding, and maintaining its own City Sector, holding it secure against the raids of the starving hordes and neighboring Sectors until all finally combined into the democratic confederation of the present City. And again Karmade thought the figures of a young man and young woman stood out briefly as he passed; the man working in the Machine Guild, designing the systems that generated food and warmth and decontaminated the City; the woman leaning over a 2-D screen in the newly formed Academy of Science and Technology. As

Karmade walked on through the time when he himself had been a child, the icons of the City's present life began to appear: the private police forces the familycorps had retained even in their City confederation; the psychtech booths, a dozen of whose psych expert systems could be remotely overseen by a single live tech like himself, and outside which City residents lined up for their five-minute diagnostic/dispensation sessions; the space colonization/exploration program, vast vehicles built in orbit to find other places for the human race to go should Earth fail at last, and to find new sources of uncontaminated raw materials—and here the Zants' personal story took over from the story of Earth. There were the space program's grueling physical, psychological, genetic, and intelligence tests, in which Nova Cloud and Irneldo Zant had scored first and second respectively. There was the hasty marriage in the midst of the Neptune mission training, and the psychoneurological compatibility surgery, in which neurological formations from various parts of their brains were cross-transplanted and stimulated to ramify, correlating their thinking processes so they could work in closer synchrony, an operation illegal for any except astronauts. There was the giant craft constructed in orbit, the launch timed to let it gain momentum from a flyby of Saturn, the two-year voyage, most of it passed in suspended animation, the pale profiles of the two astronauts rushing upward.

Then Karmade was suspended in an enormous depth, an infinite precipice falling down in every direction that his eyes recoiled from in vertigo. There was a buzzing silence. In that emptiness a speck of dust blowing from nowhere floated down the darkness. It got closer and something else came into view—the lit crescent of an enormous blue and white planet, an ocean of methane so vast it was almost as vertiginous as the emptiness in which it swam.

Then the famous story, but strangely and allegorically illustrated. The speck floated down toward a second crescent, this one Neptune's moon Triton. The picture zoomed in. Around Triton hurtled a tumbling, irregular moonlet. It crashed into the Zants' landing vehicle.

Then angels, faceless, shining creatures with vague, diffuse wings of intense light held the two astronauts, held them naked in the freezing vacuum outside their wrecked craft, that would have burst them and sent their blood sparkling away in showers of ice crystals. Nova and Irneldo swooned erotically in the angels' arms, as if Irneldo had sought in the painting to convey a lustful union with death. Then the drone craft lumbering from the mother ship to rescue them, breaking open the remains of the smashed lander, and extracting their life-support pods—

And then he saw it—something that made him start and walk two steps backward to make sure he hadn't been mistaken, and then walk back and forth watching its split-second appearance over and over until he was sure it was really there.

An eye. A single depthless black Eye staring out of the void, surrounded by a winglike field of energy.

A discreet tone sounded, making him jump, and a soft, polite voice said, "Mr. Karmade, I am sorry to interrupt your viewing of the Zant Historical Portrait, but Ms. Quasar Zant requests that you accompany her in a meeting with her guardian."

Cold anxiety blossomed in Karmade's stomach. "Why?"

"Ms. Zant asks that you be informed that Ms. Cloud meets with her once a month as a condition of her guardianship under the Zant will."

A high-grade android domestic wearing a black tuxedo walked out of the darkness of the hall. "This way please," he murmured in exactly the voice Karmade had heard disembodied.

He conducted Karmade out of the hall and to a transvator. By the time it stopped, Karmade estimated they had gone several kilometers in various directions.

The 'vator door opened and the android led him into the enormous hall of pink marble where Karmade had arrived on his first trip to Sentrex. A hundred meters away four-story arches and crimson pillars made a huge octagonal vestibule through two of whose faces the hall passed. They walked toward that, their footsteps absorbed by the enormous silence of the place.

Once they were in the vestibule, the android led Karmade toward one of the towering arches that opened at an angle to the hall and up a vast, shallow staircase of pink marble to a landing where two animals of grey stone—he thought he recognized them as lions from the TV—stood. The staircase divided and turned back a hundred meters between walls and massive carved banisters, and rose to a screen of three more huge arches. As they climbed, a vista of enormous vaulted ceilings came into view beyond the arches. At the top of the stairs the vestibule below that had seemed so gigantic was dwarfed by the arched prospects opening before them, domes merging into one another high as clouds, retreating into mysterious distances like the vaults of heaven as Karmade crossed a shimmering marble floor in the direction the android servant gestured. A chandelier the size of a thunderhead levitated halfway up to a ceiling nearly out of sight in the distance above.

He was so awed by the place that he didn't see Quasar until he almost ran into her.

Though she was as overwhelming as it in her own way; wearing a fresh white gown, her mane of black hair washed and combed, plain white earrings in her ears. But when he saw her eyes, fear filled him.

They were cold, distant, controlled; the eyes of an alter Karmade had not encountered before—but at the instant they saw him, something happened. The pale lips parted, a flush started up the icy white of the neck, and the eyes were suddenly wide, disordered—for a second something seemed to split apart, break open, and she raised her hands to her head as if to keep it from bursting. Leakage between her personalities caused by the

HED session, Karmade guessed. It looked like she had
returned to one of her most repressed personalities but
still wasn't able to completely exclude her blocked-off
memories. Even if she was in denial as to their reality—
believing them fantasies or hallucinations—they would
be terribly disturbing, and would be causing instability
in her personality structure. Ironically, such a reintegration crisis was what psych professionals treating MPDs
worked to produce; but if Ziller caught her like this,
Karmade guessed he was dead.

As with an effort of will the flush drained from
Quasar's face and the black eyes became again cold, distant, unfamiliar.

"Come this way," she said curtly. She turned and
walked. Karmade followed her.

They headed out seemingly aimlessly onto a vast desert of veined white marble. They had gone a few hundred meters when a cloud formed twenty meters above
them. Amid arbors and blooming trees an ornate throne
appeared. On the throne sat Nelda Cloud, gazing regally
out above their heads, paying no attention to them. Her
figure was slim and elegant in a long gown covered with
precious gemstones, her face smooth, unlined, young.

At her feet a little man with a big bald head was
seated at a console, half obscured by murmuring holographic readouts, his lips moving, fingers twitching at
controls. One of Nelda's lawyers, Karmade guessed.

"Aunt Nelda!" said Quasar in a bright, breathless,
freezing voice.

Aunt Nelda appeared not to have heard; her liquid
nitrogen eyes still looked out above them.

There was a short silence. Then the little lawyer said
in an impressively amplified voice: "Ms. Cloud expresses
gratification at seeing you, Ms. Zant, and graciously in-
quires as to your health and welfare; however, she wishes
to know how you have dared to allow this *person* to
accompany you, and in particular how you have dared to
allow him to touch you."

Karmade looked down in horror. Quasar's hand had

stolen into his so softly he hadn't noticed it. He snatched his hand away.

Quasar's face stayed composed, bright, freezing, as if she hadn't heard what the little man had said. If Karmade's guess was right, this personality couldn't afford to hear anything that reminded her of the sexual personality—and it was probably the sexual personality that had played the trick with the hand. Quasar's dissociated personality structure was falling apart—or rather together.

"Dr. Ziller," snapped the little man, not looking up from his console, "Ms. Cloud requires an immediate explanation of this."

A holo of Ziller appeared in the air near Nelda. "The chances of aversive conditioning such as Ms. Zant's being compromised are virtually nil. However, one of Ms. Zant's recurring delusional belief-complexes, brought on perhaps by an obsessive preoccupation with this individual, could produce the fantasy that she is able to dispense with the precautions that protect her from him. My recommendation is to dispose—"

"Ms. Cloud has not solicited your *recommendation*," snarled the little man viciously. "Mr. Rothe, Ms. Cloud wishes to know if your department has observed any conduct consistent with degradation of Ms. Zant's aversive conditioning."

"We have no clear—" began Rothe, appearing in the air next to Ziller.

Quasar laughed. It was a wild, reckless laugh, and her face was suddenly changed again, wild as a spring thunderstorm.

She kissed Karmade; a soft, clinging kiss.

Everyone was frozen. Nelda Cloud looked kindly down at Quasar for the first time.

She put her hand out with a brittle old lady's gesture that made Karmade suddenly realize her age despite the beautiful flesh that wrapped her.

"Darling." Her voice was hushed, rich, exciting. "You look feverish. Are you ill? Ziller, we must have this girl examined by the physiological people. *Thoroughly* examined."

"Under the will, you have no right to order medical tests." Quasar's voice was throbbing, melodious, uncontrolled.

"Except in emergencies." Nelda smiled, making another old lady gesture. "This is an emergency, don't you think, Ziller?"

"I will certify it as such, Ms. Cloud." Ziller sounded uncharacteristically nervous. Rothe's face was drawn, as if something terrible was happening.

"In that case, I'll use my emergency right to ask for a guardian pro tem to challenge your guardianship," said Quasar. "Rothe has the duty to honor my request."

Rage frightening in its suddenness and intensity crossed Nelda's face, making her look almost old.

"Leave us, girl," she grated.

The android domestic that had brought Karmade took Quasar's arm with a polite murmur. In a minute they were fifty meters away, heading for the screen of giant arches.

"You," Nelda rasped at Karmade. "Kneel."

The freezing hatred in her beautiful eyes almost forced him down. But something kept him standing— perhaps the trace of Quasar's kiss on his lips. He stared up at Nelda stupidly.

*"Ms. Cloud has instructed you to kneel!"* her little lawyer shouted with trembling outrage.

The holo of Rothe was wiping its face with a handkerchief.

"What has she done?" Nelda asked Karmade, her voice shaking with rage. "*Tell me.* Can she have thrown off the conditioning? Rothe, make him answer before I get angry."

"Ms. Cloud wishes to know whether you have done anything to compromise her niece's conditioning," Rothe said helplessly.

"You've been keeping us under surveillance," Karmade said. "Have you seen me doing anything like that?" That was the best nonanswer he could come up with on the spur of the moment, but to an experienced lie-detector operator like Rothe it would be as good as an admission of guilt.

Rothe's grey eyes were steely. "We found female secretions in your bedclothes this morning. Where did those come from?"

Karmade spread his hands. "You told me yourself she's had aversive conditioning against sex. Wouldn't she be having seizures if—"

"You and Ms. Zant have had simultaneous unexplained vital signs and brain field discontinuities over the past two days. What do you know about that?"

Karmade stared at Rothe. This was the worst job of lie-detector interrogation he had ever heard of. No insistence on responsive answers, spilling everything he knew before Karmade could get a word out. Not the kind of job a pro would do, unless—

He studied Rothe's drawn, pale face. And it hit him.

Rothe was on his side—or maybe on Quasar's. He was warning Karmade about what they had on him, hoping Cloud and her lawyer and Ziller wouldn't catch on.

"Nothing," Karmade said, heart pounding with the hope that he was guessing right. "I don't know anything about those things, Mr. Rothe."

"He's lying," snarled Nelda, looking down at him, and for a second he thought he saw wrinkles and wispy white hair. "He's lying, isn't he?"

"He doesn't seem to be," said Rothe slowly.

Nelda's eyes were poisonous. She opened beautiful lips twisted with hatred to say something else. But then something happened: she began to shake.

It was the helpless, Parkinsonian shaking of a very old woman, grotesque in her young body. Her eyes went out of focus. She lifted a clawed hand.

*"Bring—"* she croaked, then slumped halfway off her throne.

Half a dozen med-techs appeared from nowhere holding her limp body and attaching hoses and wires to her face and head, muttering into headsets. The hoses and wires ran to an ambulance vehicle that suddenly idled in the air nearby.

# 8

"What happened to her?" Karmade asked Rothe. The vinyl of an armchair in Rothe's dim, comfortable office felt cold, and Karmade was still trembling, as if on an instinct that Nelda Cloud's fit was more threatening to his own life than hers.

"Her anti-aging treatments," said Rothe, distractedly brushing thin fingers through his white hair. He looked as shaken as Karmade felt. "The high-powered-type treatments go that way a few percent of the time. Something about some brain chemical thrown out of whack, producing a psychotic-type state."

"Dopamine cycling," Karmade said with sudden revelation. He had heard about it, the powerful electrochemical jolt of the anti-aging treatments producing tissue damage that caused irregular bursts of dopamine overproduction and underproduction, leading alternately to dyskinesia and hyperdopaminergic psychosis. "But it's treatable. Why—?"

Rothe's hand banged down on his desk. *"Shut up,"* he snarled. "No more questions from you. No more

games. I let you get away with it in front of the old lady
and I probably saved your life. But don't think the detector wasn't going off the scale. What have you been
doing with the girl? How have you evaded our surveillance?"

Karmade watched him, trying to hold his own panic
in check. He had planned a strategy for answering the
inevitable questions during the confusion after Nelda
Cloud's fit. He had known it would take steady nerves
to go through with it; his psych training hadn't prepared
him to tangle with security professionals.

"Whose side are you on?" he asked Rothe finally, his
voice shaking a little despite his attempt to control it.

"Karmade, I'm warning you—"

"Sorry, Rothe. If I tell you anything, there's someone I want to make sure isn't going to get hurt." He
tried to meet Rothe's eyes, at the same time realizing
how ridiculous he sounded, like a character from the TV
crime shows.

Rothe glared, as if making up his mind about something. Then his voice dropped so Karmade could barely
hear him. "Suspend surveillance of my office until further notice. No, override Ziller. Confirm." In a second
he nodded, then looked back at Karmade.

"I'm not sure I like a cheap psycho doc second-
guessing me," he said with dangerous softness. "But I'll
tell you a couple of things that may help you understand.
I'm in charge of Sentrex when the old lady goes down
and I don't have that Ziller bitch running to her behind
my back all the time. But there's going to be hell to pay
when she comes out of it. *Hell to pay,* Karmade, don't
think I'm joking. Nelda Cloud, as ZantCorp delegate, is
the most powerful vote on the City Council, and nobody tells her what to do in her own private kingdom.
She's deranged at the best of times but when she comes
out of these fits she's at her worst. So everything better
be squeaky clean by the time she wakes up.

"For another thing, every move I make, and every
move everyone in Sentrex makes, is recorded by the sur-

veillance hardware this place is lousy with and transmitted to a vault somewhere—not even the old lady knows
where it is—and stored. If anything ever happens to the
girl those records go to lawyers and the City authorities,
and they get to pore over my whole career to see if I ever
once did anything raising a shadow of a doubt about my
integrity or competence. You think you could work under that kind of pressure? When you're hired to guard a
psychotic who'll try anything to hurt herself? When your
direct report is a vicious old lady who cares about nothing but keeping herself beautiful for the next couple of
hundred years?

"It's not easy at the best of times. But now I've got
to have *you* getting in my way, sneaking around with the
girl, making the old lady apoplectic.

"So it's time for you to answer a couple of questions.
Have you and the girl been evading building surveillance?"

"What if I don't tell you anything?"

Rothe shrugged. "I can work it so the wrath that
comes down when the old lady wakes up lights on you.
It would probably be kinder to kill you. But I don't want
to do that. You may not like me, Karmade, but I'm the
only friend you've got in the world right now, so you
better play along with me."

"But Quasar won't let you—"

"The girl gets medicated until we're sure she won't
give us any more trouble. Of course, we get Ziller to say
it's necessary." He shrugged. "It's happened before. It's
not nice, but I can't afford to take any more chances."

"And if I do answer?"

"If you're not hurting her, it doesn't go any further.
That's a promise. The psych people are grumbling that
she's psychologically dependent on you. 'Nonspecific
cognitive-emotive dependence,' they call it, and they
blame it on your brain-wave similarities. But that's their
problem, not mine. The way I figure it, she likes you.
I'm no brain doctor but the way I figure it, everybody
needs somebody to like, and she hasn't had anybody,

not in a long, long time. I work for *her*, Karmade, like the old lady and Ziller only pretend to. So I'm not going to break you unless I'm forced to.

"What about it, Karmade? Are you and the girl evading building surveillance?"

Karmade pretended to think. "Yes," he said finally.

"How?"

"She has some—devices her parents left her for evading surveillance."

He couldn't tell what Rothe was thinking behind his tight security operative's face. "What kind of devices?"

"Belts."

"There's not a cloaking belt in existence that can beat the high-speed, ultra-resolution imagers we have."

"These do."

"Where does she keep these belts? Where are they now?"

"No idea."

"What do you do when you're cloaked up?"

"Various things. Once we—had sex."

Rothe looked at him, then squiggled his little finger around in his ear as if to reset his earpiece. He asked the question again slowly. Karmade answered it the same way.

Rothe sat back in his chair, watching Karmade. "How does she block the conditioning?"

"Dissociation."

"Come again?"

"She's split off a separate personality that doesn't remember the conditioning."

Rothe thought for a long while. "Well, good for her," he finally said softly. "Nova, Irneldo, if you're out there somewhere—" He launched into a sudden stream of obscenities. "Imagine aversive conditioning a little *child* for God's sake. I was day shift Lead Security Operative here when they were alive. I saw her a couple of times when she came out of the sessions—once limp as a corpse, once contorted with screaming—a *baby* for God's sake, Karmade—and I wanted to—" He balled his fists and rage flashed through his tight control. "But of course I kept my mouth shut and kept getting my paycheck. No one could have made them stop. With the lawyers they had and the City officials they owned no one could have proved they were doing it, much less made them stop. So the few of us that knew just went along with it. It's amazing she's isn't any crazier than she is."

"Why is her aunt so spooked she's thrown it off?"

Rothe shrugged. "You're asking the wrong guy. There are secret clauses in the will, I know that, that only the old lady has access to, all locked up in computers and ready to bring down legal hellfire if she violates them. Maybe it has to do with one of them.

"But I don't care about that. If the girl's somehow managed to throw the conditioning off, more power to her. My job is to see that she's not hurt." He eyed Karmade. "You didn't see any signs of seizures or other problems when you—?"

"No." That was truthful; Rothe hadn't asked about what had happened later.

"What else? Your ERPs say there's something you're not telling me."

Here was where the finesse came in. To give Rothe a revelation but not the one he was looking for. "Nothing significant."

"Spill it."

"Rothe, have you ever heard of privacy rights?"

"That's something from the police shows, isn't it?"

"I'm assuring you it's nothing important."

"Then you won't mind telling me." When Karmade was silent he went on: "Karmade, I hope you're not misreading me. Sure, I'm a sensitive, caring guy; but I wouldn't hesitate a minute feeding you to the old lady. The Zant will didn't order her to keep me in this job because I'm a patsy for worn-out psych techs who think they're clever. Look, flip it around. If you tell me everything—*everything*—we'll all be cozy as bugs in a rug here. You can keep on snuggling the girl and I won't bother you. On the contrary, if it keeps her out of trouble I'll pin a medal on you, or at least get you out of here alive when she gets tired of you."

"I don't want you to get the wrong idea about her."

"I have the wrong idea about her already. Spill it."

"She thinks her parents are alive. She wants me to help her find them."

He was afraid it would backfire, that it sounded too silly for the big buildup, that Rothe would guess he was still holding something back. But Rothe looked serious, even worried. "What makes her think that?"

"I don't know."

"What do *you* think?"

Karmade shrugged.

"Has she shown you any evidence they're alive?"

Karmade studied his troubled face. "You don't really think—?"

"No, of course not."

"Then what was all that before about 'if you're out there, Nova and Irneldo'?"

Rothe laughed shamefacedly. "Nothing. We know they're dead. I saw what was left after the explosion, splattered all over their lab. Genetic tests were run to make sure it was them. No, they're dead." He sounded dissatisfied.

"But?"

"But what did they leave behind?" he said. "They were obsessed with cloaking technology. They spent most of their time cloaked and shielded so that God Himself couldn't find them. There are rumors there were inventions they kept secret, cloaks that can't be penetrated by any known technology, and now you tell me about these belts . . . What if they left other things behind—here, in this building, all around us, maybe— that we can't sense in any way? Machines, robots, androids, or even— What if they left things around the girl, for example. To protect her, or—"

"Or what?"

"To hurt her." His voice sank to a whisper. "They were crazy, Karmade. Insane."

It was late by that time. An android domestic escorted Karmade to a transvator, then down a narrow hall to his bedroom. Lying in the dark Karmade wondered fearfully if Quasar would come to him again. He had worked out an explanation during his afternoon walk for why she had chosen him for her sexual acting-out. It was known that sexual intercourse had an integrative effect on the central nervous system, neural and pheromonal entrainment loops and other links between the partners leading to intra- and inter-brain field pattern coherence. The more similar in brain functioning the partners were, the more powerful the effect. Karmade had been hired by ZantCorp because his brain functioning was by coincidence very similar to Quasar's. So in sex with him the integrative effect on her nervous system was greatly amplified. And nervous system integration was exactly what cured Multiple Personality Disorder.

Perhaps Quasar Zant's wordless sexual personality was instinctively trying to do what at least one of her other personalities had consciously decided Karmade must do using the CNS-HED machine: cure her.

Then, suddenly, she was beside his bed, gasping softly, fastening the cloaking belt around his waist, her black eyes inhuman, burning. He opened his hands to her, sobbing his terror for what would become of him. But she didn't have to cuff him this time; her unnaturally powerful hands were enough to hold him while she straddled him.

Sweat ran down her body as she rode him, wetting him where she touched.

He felt disoriented; perhaps it was some residue of Ziller's conditioning. Everything seemed far away: Sentrex, Rothe, Ziller, Cloud, even himself. Light seeped into his peripheral vision, in some hallucinatory way seeming to illuminate his body from within. It grew in intensity, washing out the solidity of the bed, the room,

Quasar's body. Quasar's flesh was faceted and glass-clear, like flawless crystal.

The light grew, the pressure of it increasing unbearably until he exploded in white light like flame.

The intense brightness slowly faded; he waited to see again. But when he did, he jerked with sudden fear of falling. He was floating above the bed, looking down on himself and Quasar twined together.

They looked dead. He thought he could smell the fetor of corpse decay, sense the rotting of their flesh.

Something else was bending over them too, a shadowy, bright figure.

He looked at it and was confronted by the Eye. Black and unblinking, close to him yet somehow remote, nested in its halo of pinkish energy.

He stared. It gazed calmly back; but he thought something stirred behind or inside it, as if it was only a cipher, a symbol for something else hidden from his sight—

Things squirmed all around him abruptly, drawing his attention from the Eye. Everything suddenly looked different; he squinted, trying to find a frame of reference that would let him make sense of the strange shapes and depths, until he realized that his surroundings had turned transparent, his vision penetrating them with a kind of clairvoyance: the bed below him, the floor and walls, the rooms beyond, the huge building, the City, Earth, space itself, and time, all rolling away on crystalline axes of multidimensional clarity.

Effortlessly he seemed to penetrate everything he looked at, an ecstatic illumination building in him; everywhere he turned his gaze he saw the insides of things, the solutions to problems, secrets.

He looked down at the woman on the bed.

There was a pattern locked inside and around her, a vast, complex vortex of forces. His gaze followed it far out into the solar system, the pattern unfolding, ramifying, enormous spaces opening out around him.

And in those spaces was a voice.

It twined upward in a wheeling, colossal silence, sin-
uously rising like incense, sweet and clear, a voice singing behind the darkness of photonic light, the gross
congestion of matter, the swarming babble of
thoughts—

He saw also that a great Being leaned over the two
figures in the Sentrex room, and that it rose up out of
Quasar's belly, as if its roots were inside her.

Karmade was aware that somewhere far away a
woman lay intertwined with a man, and she was screaming.

When he came to in his bed, the sheets soaked with
sweat, Quasar was having a seizure.

Her body shook like a broken machine, an inhuman
gurgling coming from her throat. It rose to a shriek
again and she arched hard as hot iron. He tried to hold
her, nearly insane with panic. He worked a wadded edge
of bedcover between her teeth to keep her from biting
off her tongue. Her face was knotted, inhuman. Then
she collapsed with a shuddering sob, wet and ashen,
breathing in little shaking gasps, her muscles jerking
convulsively as she lay unconscious against him. Slowly
she got quieter, hair tangled and soaked with sweat, her
body clammy and odorous with it, face troubled, a little
bloody saliva leaking from the corner of her mouth.

She needed medication, immediate medical attention; he had to turn off his cloaking belt and call Rothe.
But he hesitated. Rothe had promised to protect him *as
long as Quasar didn't get hurt*. And now she was hurt—
hurt badly—and he was partly to blame.

Quasar gave a sudden gasp and her body tensed. Her
eyes fluttered open, staring blindly at the dark.

She cried out, a wordless, terrified cry, but somehow
articulate, as if she had recovered her reason.

"Shhh. Don't be afraid," said Karmade. "Lie back
and take it easy. You need to rest."

There was a patter of running feet and Quasar jerked
up in panic.

Figures swarmed around them and they were blinded by light. Something hissing hit Karmade, crushing him against the bed. After a second of pain and confusion he realized it was a net, a resin-smelling web of superstrong threads shot from a gun. Quasar gave a grinding scream. She had been caught jumping up and the net had crushed her to her knees, twisting her head back. Stiffening and tightening as it dried, it was breaking her neck.

"Deformation patterns indicate two subjects," a clipped, professional voice said over a murmur of others.

"Lock them down and find their belts," said a voice Karmade recognized. Rothe.

Karmade's arms were pinned against his stomach. He struggled against the hardening net until he felt the two thumbplates on his cloaking belt, pressed them. Quasar's screams were cut off.

"You're killing her!" he screamed. "Stop it!"

"Solvent!" Rothe barked, and something cold and stinging hit Karmade, dissolving the net with a hiss into vapor and rubbery splatters.

Quasar had vanished.

Hard hands yanked Karmade off the bed, twisted his arms behind him. A woman ran a plastic hook down his body. It caught on something invisible above his navel.

Rothe was standing over him. "Where is she?" he demanded.

There was a yell. A security man near the door banged heavily into the wall.

"Get her," Rothe snapped. "The exits are all secured, Ms. Zant," he called.

A dozen operatives in the area of the door abruptly seemed to go crazy, sticking their arms out and running around wildly.

One of them tripped over something and two more fell over him, flailing their arms to try to grab an object they couldn't see or feel. The rest of them dived in that direction.

"Don't hurt her!" yelled Rothe, and broke into a stream of obscenities.

The operatives who had grabbed Karmade were groping around on his stomach.

"I'll get her," Karmade said to Rothe. "Call your people off. I'll get her."

"Like hell you will," Rothe snarled. "I've been sweating blood all day waiting to catch you. We found out that what we were watching in the girl's bedroom was a hologram, so I guessed she'd be here. I'm not going to let you get away again."

"They'll break her neck," said Karmade, watching the operatives stumble and flail.

Rothe cursed savagely, watching them too. Then he yelled: "Everybody freeze!"

They all stopped where they were except for one who was in the process of crashing to the ground.

"OK," Rothe snarled at Karmade. "But if you try anything I'll have Ziller electroshock you to a cinder when we find you."

One of the operatives snapped what felt like a choke collar around Karmade's neck, just loose enough for him to breathe; she held the long leash attached to it. "This operates mechanically," she told him, "so I can suffocate you anytime without interference from the cloak."

She and the others stepped away from him. It took his trembling fingers a minute to find the place where the thumb panels on the belt should be, but finally the prickling covered him and Quasar appeared crouched in a corner of the room, sobbing. Karmade walked over there, shoving an operative savagely out of his way.

Quasar was hugging herself, whether with pain or anguish he couldn't tell, rocking her body back and forth. When he touched her, she looked up with eyes that held a terrible hopelessness.

"How did they find out about the belts?" her catching voice asked. An articulate personality seemed to be back, at least.

"I told them."

She gritted her teeth and sobbed desperately, at the far shores of isolation and despair.

"I had no choice," he said lamely.

She didn't look at him, gave no indication she had heard. The roomful of security operatives stood staring blankly in their direction like a deaf and blind audience at the final episode of a wretched soap opera.

"There's nothing we can do now," Karmade said. "They won't hurt you. They—"

"With the belts," she said, fighting for control, "they can find everything—*everything* my parents left me. I'll have no place to hide. They'll own me like they own everything else."

The collar around his neck tightened slightly. "Karmade?" came Rothe's voice. "Karmade, I'll give you one more minute."

Karmade grabbed at the collar but couldn't loosen it.

"I guess we didn't fool them so good after all," he rapped, trying to smile and failing. "Rothe promised not to interfere if I told him what was going on. I guess he was lying. I—I pretended it was just the belts and that you thought your parents were alive. I didn't tell him any more than that, just that you thought your parents were alive," he answered her horrified look. "I made it sound like it was part of your delusional—"

The collar tightened so he could barely breathe. He clawed at it.

"Come on, Karmade." Rothe's voice was threatening.

Karmade was bigger and stronger than the sobbing woman at his feet, and animated by desperation; he had enough breath left to hold her down and turn off her belt by force. He made a convulsive move toward her, then stopped, gaping.

At his move she had thrown her arms over her head in a gesture of fearful submission, a gesture that suddenly filled him with the knowledge that she would never recover from such a last betrayal, never come out of the long slide into insanity it would bring on. He stood staring, a final shred of sorrow paralyzing him.

"Kill him," said Rothe, and the collar cut off breath and blood.

He seemed to be looking up from the bottom of a deep black well. He couldn't breathe and his head pounded. Everything seemed unreal. He wasn't surprised when a crack opened in the air, like a door into nothing. Something slid from the black hollow behind it, tumbling down in slow motion almost on top of him. It was a beautiful naked woman—Quasar Zant. She was dead, her head twisted hideously, her neck broken. Then three multijointed metal arms reached out of the nothing behind the door that had opened in the air, reached toward another Quasar, this one alive and kneeling by the bedroom wall, gasping and staring. She screamed and struggled as two of the arms clamped onto her wrists, but a puff of mist blew out of the opening into her face, and she went limp. The arms pulled her into the rectangle of nothing. Then the rectangle closed, so that there was only the bright room and the distant, very distant hustle and shouts of the security operatives before everything went black.

# 9

Soft, soothing blackness, the hush and thump of Mother's heart, warmth, and weightless comfort. Karmade was tired. He had been tired it seemed forever, all of him aching for sleep.

But whispering voices murmured in his ears. "Tell us everything, everything," they said, keeping him awake. "Hold nothing back, and we'll let you sleep; nothing will hurt you, nothing will wake you. Tell us what you are hiding and we'll leave you alone, leave you to sleep—tell us and you will sleep." Every part of him hurt, poised above the soft black abyss the voices kept him from. It had been going on for days, maybe years, as long as he could remember. He couldn't even remember why, when he had told the voices everything else, he was saving the one thing, keeping it from them. He opened himself to disgorge it, tell it to them so they would leave him alone, let him sleep, but then there was a small, hissing voice, like a knife cutting his brain, saying, *"No."*

*"Do you ever want to see her again?"* it hissed. *"You must not tell them the one thing. You must hide it."*

See—who? His whole life had been an agony of yearning for that velvet dark. He didn't want to see anyone, hide anything. He wanted to rest, sleep. And the murmuring voices were starting again, "Tell us everything, everything—"

He opened himself.

*"You must not tell them the one thing,"* said the small, hissing voice. *"Hide it, just one more time."*

Just one more time. He remembered that voice, the small, hissing voice, that he knew came from somewhere different than the murmuring voices, telling him that so many, many times, as far back as he could remember, foiling the murmuring voices over and over. It was absurd. He wanted to sleep. The murmuring voices were promising, "—we'll leave you alone, leave you to sleep—"

He opened himself.

The small, hissing voice spoke a name then, and it was absurd. He wanted to rest, sleep. But the name expanded in concentric circles like a stone dropped into a pool, and a vague discomfort came, as though he had forgotten something it was important to remember, and for a moment, just a moment, it came to him that the murmuring voices were lying, and then he remembered—

Then they increased the entrainment amplitude in the electrodes on his head and he sank into darkness and forgetfulness again.

But the next time, instead of pulling him slowly back up just to the level of consciousness where he could hear the voices but not remember why he was resisting them, they let him rise through it, his head clearing like a bubble expanding as it rises from the bottom of a murky pool, until he heard the hatch of the sensory deprivation chamber open, and two voices outside like blocks of ice grating against each other.

"—throwing away our best chance, Ziller," snarled the first voice. "He's still holding back on us. A little while longer and he'll crack."

"He is beginning to show signs of deterioration," said the other voice, neutral and dull. "Ms. Cloud has given strict instructions that he not be damaged. He must be capable of experiencing acute pain and despair when she is strong enough to interview him."

"But he may know—"

"I will also remind you that Ms. Cloud has now given final authority in security matters to me. I can only regret that she didn't come out of her coma earlier."

"*But the girl may not be dead*, Ziller. Didn't you hear him talking? Some kind of supercloaked device dropped a clone in there and took her—"

There was silence as hard hands pulled Karmade from the thick, lukewarm water, detached the electrodes from his head.

He had been in the interrogation tank many hours. He was too weak to stand; the operatives who had pulled him out laid him on a table and toweled him off. In his blurry vision two figures faced each other. The larger one seemed aghast, its head reared back.

"You—she wouldn't do that," said Rothe hoarsely. "Suppress evidence it was a kidnapping so she can inherit—"

"*That's enough*," hissed Ziller. Then her voice became neutral and reasonable again. "There is no evidence of such a 'kidnapping,' except in your mind. There was a *murder*, which you permitted by allowing your personal feelings to affect your judgment. Everyone regrets it, of course, but we cannot allow ourselves the luxury of a delusional escape from reality. Quite clearly this psychotic is decompensating his guilt over breaking Ms. Zant's neck by hallucinating that he saw her 'taken into the air.' But he will be in no position to entertain that opinion—or any other—after Ms. Cloud is strong enough to receive him. I'm sure Ms. Cloud would be very disturbed to learn that one of her own employees—in fact, the same one responsible for Ms. Zant's death—is maintaining a similar delusion."

There was another silence, that Ziller's voice finally broke: "Do we understand each other?"

"Yes," mumbled Rothe.

In that second Karmade remembered the one thing he had held back from them in the hypnointerrogation: his and Quasar's visit to the Warren-Hole.

Hours later the door of the small, brightly lit cell where they had put Karmade slid aside and Ziller came in. She was wearing an ill-fitting brown pants suit. Karmade had been lying on the cot that was the room's only furniture, still naked, hands cuffed behind him, his mind a welter of fear and confusion. Now he sat up dizzily, his heart, which had not stopped pounding since he had come out of the interrogation tank, deafening him.

Ziller studied him for a minute. Then she said in her muddy voice, "Mr. Karmade, I perceive your affective disturbance, and I can assure you that it is an appropriate reaction to your life situation. The gravity of your position can hardly be overstated. *Ms. Cloud wishes to personally interview you.*"

She paused as if to let that sink in. "However, because of the extraordinary character of the current circumstances, I have interceded with Ms. Cloud. I have with difficulty convinced her that she should sacrifice her own gratification for the higher good. I have wrung a commitment from her to allow me to disposition you quickly and painlessly *if and only if you cooperate fully with ZantCorp's investigation of Ms. Zant's apodosis.* If you do, you have my word that Ms. Cloud will not see you."

"You'll—you'll kill me?" Karmade rasped. "Is that what you mean?"

"Quickly and painlessly," Ziller reassured him. "It will be like falling asleep."

"But I don't want to—I don't want to—" A sob choked him.

"Mr. Karmade," said Ziller gently, "as you and I

know from our training, life is no more than a series of selections by the organism between alternative psychomotor reactions when presented with stimuli. One indicium of a mentally healthy individual is his continued ability to make adaptive selections even when every alternative seems less than ideal. In this case, I can vouch for the fact that the alternative I have presented is by far the least dysrewarding—"

"But I don't know anything! I don't know what happened to her! I don't know! I don't know!" He was sobbing now in terror, struggling against his handcuffs.

"Your performance is very impressive," said Ziller after a moment's listening to her earpiece. "And, if I may say so, not surprising after the amazing facility you exhibited in resisting our hypnointerrogation. If we had the luxury of time in which to study your technique, or a lengthy hypnointerrogation session in which to penetrate it, I would much prefer that. But as you must know —for you are familiar with the supercloaked room containing the CNS-HED and its internal records, are you not?—time is quickly running out."

"I won't tell you anything! I want to live! I want to live even if I have to talk to—to *her*."

Ziller studied him curiously for a minute. "Can it be," she said then, "that you are unaware of Ms. Cloud's—predilections? Didn't you speak to Mr. Rothe or Ms. Zant about her, ever?"

When there was no answer she went on gravely. "Mr. Karmade, I will use technical language because I know you will understand me. You are probably not familiar with the mechanics of the Morx Neurophysiological Age Reversal Regime. Few people are; MorxCorp has taken great pains to keep the procedure a secret. Without going into detail, let me inform you that a rare side effect of the procedure is progressive lesioning of the frontal and temporal lobes of the brain. Ms. Cloud is unfortunately one of the fewer than two percent of Morx patients who suffer from such lesions—lesions that have permanently affected dopamine production in these regions, resulting in cyclic overproduction and underproduction, and other related effects. You witnessed one of the results of the underproduction phase—a tardive dyskinesia-like syndrome where Ms. Cloud loses control of her musculature. But after the underproduction phase comes the overproduction phase, Mr. Karmade; do you know what that means?"

"Schizophrenic hyperdopaminism," he said. He had stopped sobbing, watching her with hypnotized intensity. His teeth were chattering. "Paranoid type."

"Excellent," said Ziller with shallow heartiness. "You are still in a rational state of mind, Mr. Karmade, very fortunately for you. Ms. Cloud's particular case presents with powerful delusions of grandeur and extreme depersonalization, which she decompensates prodromally by setting herself up as an object for the adoration of the masses and, in her acute stage, by obsessive reenactment of a para-religious ritual that most people would find—extremely distasteful. She is in her acute stage now, Mr. Karmade, and it is as such that she wishes to see you."

"But—but it's treatable. Hyperdopaminism, with the hardware you've got here, easily—even neuroleptic drugs—"

"Ms. Cloud does not wish to be treated," said Ziller. "And there is no one in the City who can compel her, or wishes to try." She paused, and her voice dropped. "Ms. Cloud has nearly compelled me to surrender you to her ritual. If I am forced to report anything less than complete cooperation on your part—"

"But I don't know anything. Please believe me. Check your lie detector. I don't—"

"Mr. Karmade, be reasonable. We know you are in possession of some method for thwarting the detectors; we learned this in our earlier encounters with you. So we—"

"There was a voice! But I don't know where it came from! I can't thwart anything! You've got to believe—!"

She studied him with her muddy eyes. Then she got

up, a short, grey-haired figure in a brown pants suit, and went out of the cell without glancing back, leaving the door open.

Another figure appeared in the doorway. A large, unclothed android with reddish, rubbery skin, a crudely formed face, its body like a muscular man's but without genitalia.

Karmade screamed, fighting the dyscontrol of terror.

After his scream had died away a distant tinkle of laughter sounded from somewhere outside the door, a light, exciting sound, lovely, like a bell of precious metal ringing.

The android took Karmade by the arm with its machine-strong hand.

It manipulated something behind his back and his hands came free from the cuffs. It dragged him out of the cot and through the door.

The door opened on a small amphitheater with seats surrounding a low, brightly lit stage. On the stage was a big surgical table with wrist and ankle straps, medical machines hung around and over it in a thicket of tubes and wires. Another reddish android was mopping something off the table, something thick and dark with a smell like hot metal that made Karmade's gorge rise.

Blood.

He averted his face as the android dragged him past the table, squeezing his eyes shut and staggering along so his arm wouldn't be pulled out of its socket.

The android dragged him through a door in the other side of the amphitheater.

Beyond was a small, luxurious anteroom with ancient wooden screens, flowering plants in pots, and a white chaise lounge now stained where the beautiful form of Nelda Cloud lay. Her perfect, ivory-smooth body was covered with a suit of wet crimson, white flecks of fat and splintered bone in it. Her eyes were closed, lips parted in ecstasy, chest heaving. There was a sound of running water. Another android was mopping the blood off her with water-soaked towels.

But even more terrible was the thing next to her.

It was a machine, a squat, intricate mechanism that made a quiet, rhythmic sound like a heartbeat. Tubes and wires ran from it to something mounted on top of it with clamps.

The thing was a severed human head, its face grotesquely distorted by the truncation of the neck muscles, the tubes and wires from the machine running into its neck and scalp. And Karmade saw that *it was still alive*, the eyes moving crazily in different directions, lids blinking mechanically.

Before he fainted, he recognized the bony face and white hair of Tom Rothe.

He woke up what seemed an eternity later, the android holding him painfully under his armpits. Nelda Cloud's eyes were a little open, and when the android pulled Karmade close to her they fluttered wide and looked at him.

She sat up eagerly and grabbed him by the forearm, leaving sticky brownish fingerprints.

He pulled away in reflexive terror, leaned over and vomited.

She giggled. She scrambled up and stood next to him, caressing his buttocks and stomach and genitals as he vomited. He tried to shrink away but the android held him. She stuck her hot, lithe tongue in his ear.

"Are you next?" she breathed, her voice exciting and intimate, as if they were in bed together. "Your lives are so small. I have to eat so many of you to be satisfied."

She kissed him tenderly.

She said to the android. "Prepare him for me."

She lay back down, chest heaving again, staring excitedly at Karmade as the other android patiently wiped a wet towel down her legs.

The first android pulled him back out into the amphitheater. He saw now the guillotine device at the head of the table on the stage. He tried to sit down on the floor, moaning in animal terror, but the android dragged him forward.

"Bring him here. Bring him to me," said a dry, calm voice. Ziller was sitting in a seat in the amphitheater.

The android hesitated a moment, then pulled Karmade up the aisle to her.

"Go," she said to it. "Leave us, both of you." The android let go of Karmade, and it and the one that had been cleaning the table went into Cloud's anteroom without a backward glance.

Ziller studied Karmade with her muddy, neutral eyes. He was sobbing, shaking his head.

"You see," she said in a low voice. "In Ms. Cloud's delusional system the ritual she performs here keeps her eternally young. Electrodes transmitting stimulation from her subject's pain centers to her pleasure centers add plausibility to her interpretation.

"But possibly you think I am bluffing, that we will keep you alive in order to preserve an indispensable information source. Please be aware that we will be able to interrogate you after Ms. Cloud's ritual. We can keep your head alive indefinitely and attach air systems that will allow you to talk. Your head can still feel pain—very intense pain, since we can stimulate the truncated efferent nerves directly. We find that the decapitated product is in fact easier to interrogate than the same head attached to a body. We believe it is a function of what you might call morale, some kind of physiological self-esteem factor that collapses when the body is gone. The only problem is timing: it takes time for the personality to stabilize enough after decapitation for interrogation to be possible; since we need to know quickly Ms. Zant's exact destination, we would rather you spoke to us voluntarily now. As I promised before, if you do we will disposition you quickly and painlessly."

"But—destination?—I don't know anything about that! I don't know!"

Ziller watched him patiently, dully.

"You flat-affect, schizoid bitch!" he screamed into her face. "She's a psychotic murderer and you're an accessory! You're an accessory, you—!"

"Ms. Cloud is the most powerful person in the City,
Mr. Karmade," said Ziller flatly. "Cooperation with her
has a far higher survival value than the converse. Fur-
thermore, Ms. Cloud's activities are not illegal. We are in
the deepest Sentrex subbasement shaft here; it extends
into the Boundary Zone, though it is of course sealed to
prevent contact. As you know, the City's legal jurisdic-
tion does not extend into the Boundary Zone. Thus,
Ms. Cloud's activities do not violate any City law. Now,
please tell me what you know of Ms. Zant's plans."

"Plans? I don't even know if she's dead or—"

"Or what?" She paused while he tried desperately to
think of an answer. "What power do *they* have to return
to the surface?"

"Who? The—"

"Let us not waste time, Mr. Karmade. Ms. Cloud
will be ready for you shortly. As I told you, the cloaking
belt we took from you allowed us to find the hidden
room and its contents, so we know *they* are down there.
Are they planning to return? If so, when?"

"I don't know." He closed his eyes. The amphitheater was spinning around him. *"I don't know."*

"I will leave you," said Ziller. "Please consider well,
Mr. Karmade. Unless you cooperate, you will be lying
on that table in just a few minutes. Think quickly; when
Ms. Cloud's parasympathetic excitation passes a certain
threshold she will take you whether I agree or not."

She got up and walked across to Nelda Cloud's anteroom door, disappeared through it.

Karmade stood paralyzed, terror draining his consciousness. He thought there was a noise and he staggered around woozily, but the place was silent, empty
except for a big plastic bag like a garbage bag lying next
to the table on the stage, with something bulky in it.

A hissing voice said in his ear, *"The bag."*

He spun around again. The amphitheater was still
empty. The hallucinatory voice, the same voice in his
head that had made him resist the hypnointerrogation,

was yammering at him, urging him desperately to do something he didn't dare do or even think about—

*"The bag! The bag!"*

He stared at the plastic bag. The thought of what must be in it made his gorge rise and his heart pound.

*"You must!"*

He forced himself to move tremblingly to the bag. He didn't want to touch it. His hands shook uncontrollably and nausea darkened his eyes.

*"Now! You must!"*

Nelda Cloud's anteroom door was closed.

Maybe there was no surveillance of this place; maybe Nelda Cloud was sane enough not to want the evidence of her crimes recorded along with everything else that went on in this building.

He loosened the bag's drawstring, pulled it open. The smell and sight of the shockingly mutilated thing inside made him retch.

He closed his eyes and dragged it out by its armpits.

It was heavy as stone. Cool blood squeezed out of clots and ran down his chest and legs as he dragged it.

*"Yes. Yes—"*

He dragged it up the aisle between the amphitheater seats, let it slump to the floor behind the last row.

Then he ran back and curled up inside the bag himself, pulling it clumsily over his head, tightening the drawstring as much as he could from inside, nearly fainting from the overpowering stench of blood and feces that stained the plastic around him.

He had barely finished when a door slid aside.

They had seen him. They had caught him.

Footsteps came near and hands took hold of the bag, tightened the drawstring, and seemed to tie it. Then the bag was lifted.

Karmade didn't breathe, tried to be dead.

He was carried with mechanical strength; there was no sound of breath; it was an android.

It stopped walking and a door hushed aside. It went in and there was a surge of gravity—a transvator going up. The android got out and its feet shuffled on bare concrete. It stopped three times for doors that hissed like decon locks. After the third they were in a place that sounded small.

There was a faint tapping, like a keypad.

Then a humming and vibration, a hollow metal clank. Karmade got tossed onto something hard and then the humming boomed around him much louder and he felt metal opening under him.

It was a garbage chute. He dropped into black space and then cold water.

He tumbled over and over in a swift current, breathing the last pocket of air in the bag before it bubbled out the opening. He thrashed to turn the bag over so he could gasp another breath, but he could barely move inside it. He tried to kick his way out, couldn't. His chest was about to explode. Everything was going black.

He vaguely felt the cold thickness of water in his lungs.

The dizzy rushing of water cleared itself suddenly in his ears, stretching out in all directions through the darkness.

He guessed idly that this was death.

# 10

Karmade woke a long time later to shades of grey and gritty textures, low squawking sounds, and a nagging, feverish ache in his chest.

He lay still until his eyes focused. It took him a few minutes then to figure out that instead of a cell or interrogation chamber or hospital room, he was lying in a cave. Someone was facing away from him in a rocking chair and watching a tiny 2-D TV propped on a broken-down night table.

The rocking chair went back and forth with a slow, regular creak. Karmade's head weighed a ton as he lifted it. He lay on a cot. Under his blankets he was wearing patched grey clothes. They seemed tolerably clean, though damp with his sweat.

There was a cracked child's bureau in a corner of the cave and a dirty, worn rug in front of that. The cave was lit by a fragment of illumination tile stuck into the hard dirt of the ceiling. The walls were hard dirt too, except on one side where there was only darkness.

Karmade lay for a long time wondering dully where

he was, his body throbbing with what felt like ebbing fever. Then he heard something he recognized in the low squawking from the TV.

"—Theodore Karmade, for whose capture ZantCorp Systemwide is offering a reward of ten billion dollars—"

His picture was displayed on the screen.

He didn't move but perhaps the person in the rocking chair heard his breath, because he turned around.

"You're on TV," he said when he saw Karmade looking at him, and cackled with laughter.

He was old. His skin was an unhealthy pink under a layer of dirt, with crude tattoos on his wrinkled cheeks. One of his rheumy, pale blue eyes hung far open showing the wet pink inside the socket, as if he had been badly injured sometime. He had broken teeth and a sparse white beard straggling off his chin.

A sewer tribe man.

He got up stiffly and stood over Karmade. His patched clothes had once been a business suit, probably scavenged from some City trash heap. His hands were blue-veined and wrinkled, with long, yellow fingernails.

"—responsible for the murder of megatrillionaire beauty Quasar Zant, news of whose death has set off a wave of public disturbances, religious demonstrations, looting, and suicides. City psychologists connect this behavior—"

"Did you do it?" rasped the sewer tribe man, leaning over so that Karmade caught his greasy, unclean smell. "Did you kill her? Why did you do it?" His bloodshot eyes gleamed eagerly and his coarse, thick lips were drawn back in a grin.

Karmade shook his head.

"You been screaming for her," the old man said. "In your sleep."

Karmade looked into his leering eyes.

"The shaman woman says her ghost is calling you, and that's why you scream."

Karmade closed his eyes, trying to find his way through a maelstrom of feelings.

When he opened them someone was standing next to the old man, someone tall and stooped wearing black robes worn thin and ragged, eyes sunk deep into a thin, wrinkled face, dirty grey hair growing around a bald spot on the top of her head.

The two of them stared down at him.

"Where am I?" Karmade asked finally, his voice thick and dry. He knew that pockets of tribespeople lived in the sewers and tunnels above the Boundary Zone all over the City, at various depths. He could be anywhere from a few meters below the streets to hundreds of meters down.

"What do you care about that?" asked the old man. "Underground; you're safe."

"Are you—?"

"Ur-people," said the man, and a flicker in his watery eyes warned Karmade not to say 'sewer tribe.' "Not mutants." His eyes flickered again.

"How did I—how did I get here?"

The old man looked at the old woman. She was still staring at Karmade. The old man said slowly, "Our people found you in the sewer, in a bag. We saved you from the uppy soldiers. They're looking for you. If it wasn't for us, they would have you now."

"Did you kill her?" the old woman asked. "Quasar Zant?"

Her voice was hoarse and old, but strong. There was something young about her. Maybe it was her eyes, or the sudden impression of vigor she gave when she spoke. Or maybe she *was* young, the biocide burden she had built up living outside the City's decontaminated environment aging her prematurely. It was said that the sewer tribespeople's life expectancy was half that of the average City dweller.

"No. I don't think so," Karmade said.

"We could get ten billion dollars for him regardless," the old man said without much hope. "The news says. Our whole clan could move up to the surface, get decontaminated, live in a rich building—"

She ignored him. "But you knew her," she said to Karmade.

"Yes, I—I knew her."

"She healed you," said the old man, nodding at the old woman. "You had the sewer infection bad. She gave you medicine. If it wasn't for her—"

"Be quiet, you babbling old man," said the woman. "Sit down and watch your screen if you can't stop talking."

The old man looked sheepish, then sat in his rocking chair with his back to them, grumbling faintly.

"Who killed her if you did not?" said the old woman. "The Old One?"

"You mean Cloud? Her aunt?"

She nodded.

"I don't know—I don't think anyone killed her. Someone—took her. Kidnapped her." Karmade didn't know why, but he trusted this old woman as he hadn't trusted anybody since he had gone into Sentrex. In any case, there didn't seem to be much choice but to answer her questions.

"The Old One?"

He shrugged. "Why did you save me?"

The old woman gave a little shrug of her own. "At first they thought the bag you were in held the remains of one of our people. Then when we saw the news we shielded you."

"You're not going to—" He swallowed and looked at the TV, where a hysterical teenager was being interviewed about Quasar Zant's death.

"Perhaps not," said the old woman. Then she turned and walked out of the cave, black robes fluttering.

When she was gone the old man got up and stood looking down at Karmade again with impatient curiosity.

After a while the old man brought a battered pan of water from somewhere and gave Karmade a sponge bath, his hands surprisingly deft and gentle. A muscular, dead-pale young man with long, matted hair had appeared silently at the open end of the cave, watching Karmade steadily as the old man worked, squinting in the dim light. He looked like a fourth- or fifth-generation tribesman.

"How—how long have I been here?" Karmade asked as the old man threw his sweat-stained shirt into a corner and sponged cool water over his chest and arms.

"You ain't been here long, but you're a lot better off than when we found you. You had a high fever. *She* put spells on you to pull you back."

Washing done, Karmade felt much better. The old man helped him into a clean, ragged jumpsuit. Then he and the young man lifted Karmade out of the cot and into the rocking chair. The old man went away and brought back a big, steaming bowl of dark, rich broth, which he helped Karmade eat, sitting on his haunches next to the chair. He had to hold the spoon; Karmade's hand trembled too much. The broth was salty and delicious, strengthening.

"What is this?"

"Rat," the old man said. Karmade didn't know what that was but he ate eagerly until the bowl was empty.

The TV was still on, turned down low. While the old man took the bowl away, Karmade watched it, sitting weakly back in the chair.

"—lying in state in the Grand Hall of the Zant Sentrex Building, where dignitaries, celebrities, and City residents have gathered to pay their last respects to this young woman, the only survivor of the City's greatest familycorp, whose life was so bound up with the deepest aspirations of the City, as if she herself were its soul—"

A crowd that looked a million strong filled a vast space, weather booms arching a kilometer above, walls and domed ceiling lost in a silvery haze. The camera cut to somber-faced dignitaries filing past a crystal coffin set with gemstones of deepest red, blue, green, and purple, laid on a white stone table in a sea of flowers—fresh, real flowers that must have denuded all the gardens in Sentrex, and worth more than all the money in the City—and in the coffin a face more beautiful than all the flowers and gems, paler in its repose than the white stone.

"—hearings regarding the circumstances of her death, including a review by City officials and a team of attorneys of stored data from monitoring equipment that kept track of her every move and those of her caretakers, as mandated in secret provisions of Irneldo and Nova Zant's will never before revealed, and whose implementation was triggered by the killing—"

The camera panned up a massive marble pillar that rose high above the crowds and coffin. Sitting at the top on a marble throne, surrounded by attendants, sat a slender figure in pure white gowns. A lacy veil covered her face, and as Karmade watched, heart pounding in fear and loathing, a long ivory hand dabbed a lace handkerchief at the eyes hidden behind it.

There was a snarl that made him jump, and the old man, who had appeared silently beside him, spat savagely on the floor. The young man's wide-eyed face was twisted with fear.

"Demon!" the old man hissed. "Her tears are ice, her sobs belches of man-flesh—

"Her soldiers hunt us for her appetites," he hissed at Karmade when the camera was panning the crowd again. "We find what is left of them in the sewers, just like we found you."

"—deep sorrow at Quasar Zant's murder, blames a negligent security chief for lax safety measures and indulging her niece's obsession with a deranged psychiatric technician Ms. Cloud had earlier dismissed—"

The announcer's hushed voice was suddenly cut off as the camera continued to scan the crowd. In a few seconds another voice came on, this one deep, authoritative, excited.

"We regret to interrupt our coverage of this solemn event to bring you an exclusive news flash. A massive explosion in the City's 4th Sector in the last hour has damaged a large section of the Utopia Apartment Complex, *and City officials are now saying the explosion appears to be a breakout attempt by mutants from the underground city.*" The picture cut to a confused, jostling night scene of heads and shoulders, and beyond them the wall of a slum tenement with orange flames pouring from a jagged hole at ground level. A squad of Boundary Guard troops—a phalanx of android soldiers followed by their human operators in combat armor—suddenly rushed between the camera and the flames, the unsteady picture zooming onto them.

"The City has imposed a curfew in the Sector and mobilized a Boundary Guard division to isolate the breach. City spokesmen urge calm and say that no mutants appear to have escaped. Automated construction crews have already begun to repair the breach area, and the Boundary Guards have taken punitive measures, pumping poison gas and biological agents down the hole created by the explosion—"

The old man standing next to Karmade murmured a magic charm.

Karmade's trembling, which the hot broth had eased, was now back in full force, and his teeth chattered.

The old man looked down at him with sudden worry. "What's the matter? You cold? Oh, hell." He and the young man helped Karmade back from the chair to the cot. "If you get sick again that old hag'll skin me. Come on, lie down and sleep. Don't start tearing at yourself again, or we'll have to tie you down. And don't scream; I have to sleep too, you know."

And he did sleep, on the floor of the cave without a blanket or pillow, snoring so loudly it didn't seem any amount of screaming could wake him, the illumination tile turned down low so that Karmade could barely see the outline of the rocking chair.

For a long time Karmade lay awake. His ears hissed and he alternately shivered and sweated, he guessed with the remnants of the sewer fever. His thoughts were a jumble, his mind running obsessively over the things that had happened to him, trying to remember them clearly, fit them into the right order, make the connection between them and the person he had always thought he was. A feeling of wonder came over him at his escape from Sentrex, and the feverish conviction that someone or something had guided him at the crucial moment, the hissing voice that had driven him to get into the body bag.

Random images swirled through his brain. He found himself thinking of Quasar lying beautiful and chill in her coffin surrounded by flowers and a million people, and tears welled out of his eyes.

The feverish rushing in his ears became louder. "... *not dead* ..." it seemed to hiss.

He listened, suddenly afraid. The darkness was dull and unmoving, the silence torn by the old man's snores.

"Hello?" Karmade quavered finally. "Who is it?"

"... *not dead. Find her* ..." a definite voice hissed.

He jerked in panic, twisted around, and strained his eyes into the dark to see if anyone was there. The voice fluttered and got garbled, as though his movement had disturbed the fever hallucination.

A distant noise echoed in the darkness, as if through long tunnels. It sounded like gunfire.

The old man's snoring suddenly cut off and he was standing silent and tense as sprung steel, turning the knob on the illumination tile so that the blackness became complete. After a minute Karmade couldn't tell if he was still there; he made absolutely no sound.

Karmade lay back again and fever-shapes took form before his eyes so that he cringed in fear, thinking he saw now a leering mutant, now a murderous Zant soldier leaning over him. The distorted whispering faded in and out.

"—*enough time* ... *wants to destroy* ... *die soon if* ... *go*—"

Other whispering, even fainter, came from where the

old man had been standing. Karmade's cot rose off the floor. He made a small sound of fear and surprise.

"Quiet," the old man breathed in his ear. "We are moving you. Someone has found us."

Then there was no sound but air hissing past. The cot jogged with his bearers' running. Soon it tilted and he thought they were going downward.

A burst of machine-gun fire, distant but unmistakable, echoed through cavernous darkness. The jogging of the cot got more violent.

Air hissed past again. Gunfire sounded once more, but very far away, an echoing whisper.

There was the faint scraping and shutting of a door. Then someone turned up an illumination tube.

In the dim, greenish glow the old man and young man who had carried Karmade stood gasping and sweating. The old man peered at him closely, then went and murmured to someone else.

Karmade could see a little of the place they were in. There was a rough, grimy floor and huge, rusted wheelworks with enormous pipes that ran up into darkness. He couldn't see ceiling or walls. The place had a sour, dusty smell. A dozen people stood near one of the huge pipes. Karmade recognized the old shaman woman he had seen before. Another of them, a square-jawed man with tangled, shoulder-length grey hair, came and looked at Karmade with eyes that glinted like steel in the half-light. Then he rejoined the others.

They argued in voices too low for Karmade to hear. After a few minutes they split up, some of them hurrying into the darkness, four coming to stand over him, two men and two women. Among them was the black-robed old woman.

She stayed silent as one of the others, the steely-eyed man, questioned him: "You must answer me quickly and truthfully if all of us are to stay alive. Do the uppies know where you are?"

"I—I don't know—how could they?"

"Are you carrying any kind of device, transmitter, that would let them find you?"

Karmade's heart started to pound, fear increasing his dizziness. "No—no, I don't think so. How could they have—?" He stopped, realizing how foolish it was to think that Rothe or Ziller would not have planted a device to keep tabs on him in Sentrex, through his food perhaps, or by injection when he was unconscious—a device that was probably blasting out a homing signal to the ZantCorp soldiers.

The steely-eyed man looked at the old woman, but she was watching Karmade with stony impassivity.

"Did you touch Her when you were with Her, up in Her palace? Did you touch Her?" the old woman asked.

"Yes."

"Where is She now?"

"I don't know. Dead, maybe."

"Then who have you been speaking to when no one is there?" The old woman's eyes were shadowed.

"I heard—a voice a few times," he said. "The fever perhaps—a hallucination."

"What did the voice say?"

"I—I don't know."

The steely-eyed man snorted. The old woman raised her eyes to him and he looked away.

"What do you want of us?" the old woman asked Karmade.

He stared at her in surprise but she was impassive, the others around her watching him tensely. The sewer tribes had no love for City dwellers, he knew, they themselves being the City's rejects, the descendants of criminals, dissidents, and unproductive workers, driven from the decontaminated surface by poverty and other pressures.

The steely-eyed man burst out: "Kaleth, whatever he wants, we must *get rid of him!* He is leading the uppies to our encampments. You know what they will do if they find us."

"What do you want of us?" the old woman asked Karmade again.

"Are you mad? Do you want the Old One to have our children? Do you—"

"He has touched Her," said the old woman. "Their fate grows strong down below. The times are changing; I have heard it. Do you understand? I have *heard*. Do you want to sell him to the Old One when She is calling him? Or should we not all die to save him?"

"I do not mind dying, Kaleth," said the man. "But when I think of the Old One taking my little son—" He made magical gestures of protection and there was a murmur of assent from the others. "If times are changing it will be no hurt to us. We have never benefited from these times. But we must think first of our children. We will not sell him to anyone, but he must go."

"Oh, you'll turn him out sick and feverish for the uppies to hunt down as he crawls?" sneered the old woman. "How noble, Arol."

The man looked stung. One of the others, a young woman, spoke up: "Arol, there are big pipes below us that should be able to block the signal from any device he is carrying."

"For as long as he stays in them," said the man Arol. "But surely he would rather the uppies take him than live the rest of his life in a pipe."

"But we could keep him there until he is fit. Then we could take him somewhere safe in the upland. After that he would be on his own."

Arol was silent.

"I agree," said the man who had not spoken yet. "It would be no honor to send even an uppie out like this, Arol, whatever the Old One may do."

"Let's remember why we let them live down there in the first place, rather than cleansing the Earth of them during the Consolidation, as many authorities argued we should," said Rudof Sorek from Karmade's 2-D TV screen. "It was mercy and compassion pure and simple, mercy and compassion extended to them at the hour of our extremity, even though it was a luxury we could scarce afford. We let them go on breeding and mutating down there even though the terrible logic of our times said they should be scoured, even though every consideration argued that we should sterilize the Earth of them as we did every other living thing to safeguard the very survival of our species."

"But now we have found out, and not for the first time, that they are not satisfied with the gift of life we gave them. Many experts believe their mutations by now have carried them so far from anything recognizable as human that they are no longer capable of human feelings such as gratitude or honor. In effect a hostile alien race teems below our streets, scheming to break out and take over our City.

"My friends, *this City is the last refuge of the human race. We are talking about the survival of our species,* the end that justifies any and all means. We cannot afford to risk our survival—and indeed, we have no right to risk it. We must turn back these attacks and make sure there will never be another one. We must do now what we should have done one hundred years ago, and remove this threat to our lives, our race, and our world, once and for all, before it is too late."

Karmade lay propped on a pile of blankets inside a dark, two-meter metal pipe, the small TV screen dimly lighting its rusty walls. He had been in the pipe three days now, resting and watching the endless TV debates over what the City should do about two recent explosions set off by mutants in apparent bids to escape to the surface. There had been no mutant breakout attempts in nearly thirty years—and never any this big—and the City was on the verge of panic.

The camera switched to Jim Parlet, a thin man who looked like a college professor. "These are living creatures we're talking about, Mr. Sorek," he said in an unpleasant, reedy voice. "We owe them more than we can ever repay, since we're the ones who forced them underground one hundred years ago. It would be wrong to do what you suggest—simply wrong to kill them for wanting to come up out of the shelter-cities where they live on our garbage, teeming in filth, crying out against our injustice—"

Karmade had gotten the feeling, watching the debates day after day, that they were fixed, since the advocates of military action to "sterilize" the underground land always seemed to win in some subliminal, visceral way. The opponents of the military option all seemed vaguely repulsive, with whining, nagging voices, unhealthy, slightly unnatural faces. Karmade studied Parlet's greyish, crooked teeth, the complexion that looked like pimples covered with makeup. But if he was an actor or sophisticated android psychoformed to repel viewers from the opinion he espoused—that the City should investigate the explosions further before deciding to destroy the mutants—what did it mean? Probably that the City Council had exercised its emergency "accelerated constituent education" regulations to secretly place propaganda and subliminal messages in the media as it deemed necessary for the public health and safety.

Karmade had had three days to think about a hundred questions more important to his survival than the mutant debates, but for some reason—post-traumatic stress syndrome, he supposed—his brain refused to focus on his predicament. Instead he lay and watched the debates, weighing the arguments, getting to know the participants, speculating as to the outcome. He was content to tell himself that he was recuperating, and would think about his own problems later. Their strangeness and complexity made this a doubly appealing option.

"—*had* to scour the infective organisms from the Earth, as you well know, Mr. Parlet," Rudof Sorek was saying. "The biowar retrovirus plagues had already seriously penetrated the human population at that time, and if we had not acted immediately our whole race would now be splitting into hundreds of types in a catastrophic genetic divergence that would destroy us. And yes, Mr.

Parlet, I am sure our audience is well aware that the war retroviruses were engineered to self-destruct after a certain number of years, rendering the mutants no longer infective, but as *you* very well know, the corrupt genetic material could be introduced into our bloodlines in other ways, such as sexually or by laboratory engineering—"

The pipe vibrated dully under Karmade and an illumination tube came on, showing the young man—Josif —who had helped carry Karmade away from the gunfire three nights ago.

"I have brought your food." He set a small pot of broth on Karmade's lap and handed him crusts of bread that seemed to have been rescued from a garbage dump: they were dry and stale, not quite moldy. Karmade devoured all of it ravenously, Josif squatting nearby.

When he was done Josif asked politely whether he felt strong enough to walk. He helped Karmade to his feet and they walked a hundred meters down the inside of the pipe, the tube Josif held lighting clouds of brown, brackish rust their feet kicked up in the stale air, the curved walls fading ever farther ahead as they moved. Karmade was tired when they got back, and lay down as Josif faded out the open end of the pipe twenty meters away. The news was on: "—collapse of a residential block in the 9th Sector as the result of a pre-dawn subterranean explosion has brought a new urgency to the debate over planned counterattacks against the mutants, possibly signaling the beginning of a massive military campaign to sterilize the under-City areas. Questioned about the implications of such a move, City officials revealed the existence of sterilization contingency plans, and said they could be accomplished with a minimal impact on the health and safety of City residents—" the newscaster yammered as the picture showed a smoking mountain of concrete rubble laced with bent and twisted steel, a tottering cliff of wall-stripped rooms standing above it, ambulance copters lowering stretcher booms while android soldiers scrambled in the wreckage.

# 11

After his next meal Karmade was strong enough to walk all the way to a place where the pipe sloped steeply downward, disappearing into black nothingness below, and then back to his bed, a distance of perhaps half a kilometer. He turned off the TV soon after Josif had slipped into the darkness beyond the open end of the pipe, and lay in a puddle of light from the illumination tube. In a little while there was another vibration under him and a stooped figure shuffled into the pipe.

It was the old woman Kaleth.

"Are you well?" she asked in her harsh voice. "Arol wishes to know when you will be well. I am afraid he is anxious to send you away." She spat on the floor. Then she came closer and lowered herself stiffly near his feet. "He can think only of safety, as if safety to live in sewers and eat garbage were a great treasure."

"But where am I to go?" The question, which Karmade had refused to think about over the past days, came suddenly out of his mouth. "There is no place for me to go."

She shrugged. "These tunnels and sewers run everywhere between the Boundary Zone and the upland. The Ur-people can go anywhere in the City the uppies can go, and many places they cannot. If there is a safe place anywhere, Arol and his people will find it for you." She sat in brooding silence for a minute. Then she asked, "You will not try to find—Her?"

He studied her anxiously. "Quasar? What makes you think she's alive?"

"I have—heard things."

"I don't understand you," he said haltingly. "But even if she is alive, I would have no idea how to find her. Right now I'm thinking about staying alive myself."

Kaleth's bony hand came out of the folds of her robe and she pointed a clawlike finger at the floor.

"Down," she said.

"What?"

"Down. She is down, down below us."

"What—where? How do you— What makes you say that?"

"I have listened. I can *hear*, a little—things most people cannot hear."

He stared at her, stunned. "You're a telepath? A *mutant*?"

She shrugged. "I *hear*. When I was young and realized this, I came down here before I could be caught and sent someplace worse." She studied him and seemed to make up her mind about something. "I will tell you something. I have listened for many years now, listened down here to things both below and above. And I tell you there are Voices both below and above the City, powerful Voices that say someday the low will be raised up. Someday soon. There are stirrings now. Times will change." Her eyes were shadowed. "And I have heard that She is down there." She pointed again with her withered finger.

"Where? What is—down there?"

"The Warrens."

He stared, stricken. He tried to laugh but it came out

a dry, croaking sound. "That's ridiculous. What—what do you mean?"

"She is down there."

"The mutants kidnapped her? But how—?"

"Perhaps her disappearance is part of a plan. The times are changing. Perhaps the new gods down below have taken her."

"Gods?"

"Be quiet. I should not have spoken that aloud." She listened then, but there was no sound in the darkness outside the pipe. After a minute she went on, whispering: "There are things I hear that perhaps no one is supposed to know. The mutants have gods they believe are powerful enough to bring them into their inheritance—for they believe they will inherit the world above."

"Is that why they've been blasting tunnels to the surface? Are they going to attack?"

She shook her head. "The Ur people who patrol the tunnels and sewers have seen the Old One's soldiers setting the charges for the explosions they blame on the mutants."

"The Old One—Nelda Cloud? ZantCorp soldiers setting the explosions and blaming the mutants?"

She nodded.

He tried to think about that but couldn't. His head was spinning already with thoughts, fear, rage at the people who would turn him out.

She got up stiffly and stood over him, light from the tube making her eyes pools of shadow. "She is down there," she muttered, "and somehow my heart tells me she needs you.

"Let them take you there when Arol comes." She pointed. "Down."

But he was shaking his head in mute terror.

She stared at him for another minute, then turned and shuffled away down the pipe.

• • •

"—continue the intensive manhunt for Theodore Karmade, the psychotic mental health vendor wanted for the murder of celebrity goddess Quasar Zant—" the TV was yammering when he turned it on, and a full-length picture of Theodore Karmade lit the darkness. Karmade studied it wide-eyed, studied the man caught by a camera in one of the enormous Sentrex halls. A tall man in an expensive suit, who might have once been sane, even handsome. But some disorder had sunk his eyes into dark circles, stooped his shoulders, made his face haunted and fearful—

Karmade knew his psychotics. He had treated hundreds, perhaps thousands, in his psych-booth practice. The man he saw in that picture, broken under electroneural aversive conditioning, was the type who might very well fall in love with and then kill the conditioned-against stimulus, might very well repress the memory of the killing and cover it over with a hallucination that a mysterious, invisible machine had taken her away—

The thoughts and feelings that had been held back over the days of his convalescence suddenly avalanched upon him. The pit of his stomach felt as though he were falling, falling into a deep void. If he *had* killed Quasar Zant, he would have to die too; that much was suddenly clear to him. After what he had seen of himself and other humans in the last weeks, the filthy sadism and filthy pain, the hypocrisy and fear, power and cravenness, suffering and shame, rage and slaughter, there was no way for him to withstand the thought of having killed her, the one small, powerful soul who had fought against it all. Her raging black eyes, her crazy faith that her parents were alive, and her reckless contempt for her aunt were among the few handholds he had left on sanity, on the idea that anyone could oppose the rottenness he had found at the heart of the world. If he had killed her, been responsible for the obliteration of that beauty and defiance, he would have to follow her; it was like some natural law—the law of last chances.

His only hope was to know that he hadn't killed her.

But for that to be true, a machine undetectable even by the Zant supercloakers would have to have taken her. The body in the white Sentrex bedroom would have to have been a clone.

Such a clone would have to have grown for years from a sample of Quasar's cell tissue to be at the right state of development. Someone would have to have planned the abduction for years, and then have had the luck to be waiting in that bedroom in the invisible machine with the naked clone at exactly the right time.

Despair came over him. It was impossible.

Yet Ziller had interrogated him about *Ms. Zant's destination* and *Ms. Zant's plans.* Did she have some reason to think Quasar Zant was alive? *Could* someone have penetrated Quasar's supercloaker technology, watched her every move at Sentrex, planned for years to abduct her and make it look like she had died? There were only two people who had ever lived who might possibly have had the technology to do such a thing. But they were supposed to be dead too.

Yet Quasar had never believed they were dead.

Sweat came out on Karmade as he searched for a different conclusion. But he couldn't find one. For the abduction to have happened, Nova and Irneldo Zant had to be alive.

It was crazy, but there were a few possible consistencies. Quasar's supercloaking belts and the hidden Sentrex CNS-HED room seemed to indicate planning for a future where Quasar would be left at the mercy of her psychiatric caregivers and security people, at least for a while. After that maybe Nova and Irneldo had planned for her to join them.

Join them where?

A shiver went through him.

Two people as rich and powerful as the Zants would need to go into hiding under only one circumstance, as he had told Quasar. And if they *were* mutants there was only one place they could hide. The City was too full of random checks and dragnets and genetic testing; they would catch you sooner or later if you stayed there. The exoCity was too poisoned to live in, and would be for years. You would have to go to the Warrens. Maybe if you went secretly before you were caught you could take things with you: machines, food, money perhaps, if money meant anything down there.

And the Warrens was where the old shaman woman said she had telepathically sensed Quasar.

There was something else too. The old woman had said the underground explosions the TV was screaming about had been set off by ZantCorp soldiers to look like the mutants had made them. Why would ZantCorp do that? To stir up antimutant passions? To goad the City into taking action against the mutants?

Why?

Nelda Cloud's people had found the CNS-HED records in the hidden Sentrex room, Ziller had said. Had something in the records suggested to them that the Zants were hiding in the Warrens? That they might return someday and challenge Nelda's right to the money she needed to stay young and beautiful for the next few hundred years? Would the Old One rather that all the mutants died, Quasar and her parents among them, than risk that happening?

Karmade was soaked with sweat now, beginning to realize where his logic led.

He thankfully ate the meal Josif brought a little while later, then walked several times up and down the pipe with him. He slept afterward, waking when footsteps vibrated the pipe; not Josif's or Kaleth's, but firm, powerful steps. The man named Arol was leaning over him, dressed as he had been before in a patched bodysuit that might have belonged to a sanitation worker long ago.

"How are you feeling? Josif tells me you are stronger."

Karmade stared up in fearful surprise. "You're not sending me away now? I thought—"

"I'm sorry," Arol said, and he looked sorry. "The uppies have sent three expeditions into the upper tun-

nels in the past few days. We are packing, preparing to
move our encampment, but we cannot take you with us
for fear their machines will detect you. I am sorry, but
we must escort you away within the hour, while the way
is clear. You will tell us where you want to go and we will
do our best to get you there.''

He turned and walked away, out the end of the pipe.

The hands Karmade rubbed over his face shook. He
lay back and closed his eyes.

A little while later the pipe vibrated again. Into the
light came three men—Arol, Josif, and another man
Arol's age, strong and hardened, in tattered clothes,
beard, and long, tangled hair. Josif and Arol had smart
cord canisters slung over their shoulders; Arol and the
other man carried long blanket rolls.

"So," said Arol. "Where do you wish to go?"

Karmade's voice wouldn't work. His lips trembled
uncontrollably. Finally, fighting himself, he managed to
croak: "The Warrens."

The three men stared in astonishment.

"You are not serious?" said Arol. "You've been talking to that mad old woman, haven't you? Listen, don't
think you can only escape from the uppy soldiers down
there. There are places in the 18th Sector—not in the
sewers but on the surface—where fugitives live, evading
the uppies their whole lives. We can take you there."

The crimorgs were strong in the slums of the 18th
Sector, Karmade knew, but not strong enough to hide
him from a determined hunt by ZantCorp even if he had
had the money to buy their services. He shook his head.
"The Warrens," he said.

The men were silent. "May I ask why?" Arol asked
finally.

Bitterness and fear choked Karmade. He just shook
his head.

The men drew off a few paces and held a low-voiced
argument. When they came back Arol was stone-faced.

"All right," he said, "though we think it is insane.
But you must understand that our commitment is only

to take you to the entrance of the Warren-Hole, not beyond. *We* do not wish to die."

Karmade nodded mutely.

"Then let us begin," said Arol grimly.

The hard-looking man, whom the others called Lon, helped Karmade to his feet. "If you cannot walk, I will carry you," he said gruffly.

Karmade nodded. He turned toward the open end of the pipe but the man pointed in the opposite direction. "This way," he said.

They started into the pipe the way Josif and Karmade had taken on their after-meal walks, Karmade wondering where they were going; there were no openings in the pipe that way. Arol went first, a light-patch on his jumpsuit giving off a greenish glow that showed the curved walls for a couple of meters ahead. Karmade came behind Arol, Josif and Lon following. Their footsteps made the pipe thrum dully, and brownish, metallic dust rose beneath their feet.

They stopped at the place where the pipe sloped down into darkness. Arol pulled a short length of cord from his smart canister and selected a termination, a flat magnetic plate. He attached the cord and stuck the termination to the floor of the pipe, grinding it down to make sure the magnet held fast through the rust. Then he clipped on a harness, fastened it around his hips like a seat, and started walking backward down the slope, the canister giving out cord. In a little while there was a dull clunking as the harness rattled back up the pipe to stop by the termination.

Lon fastened the harness around Karmade. "Hold the grips with both hands," he said. "Turn to face me. Walk backward; don't be afraid. Can you do it? I'll carry you if you want."

Karmade started down. He could see dim greenish light coming up the pipe from below; rust particles in the air scratched his throat and eyes. It was not heavy work but by the time he reached the bottom his arms were trembling and he was gasping.

Arol helped him down the last few steps, unstrapped the harness, sent it back up. "Are you all right?"

Karmade nodded, his breathing echoing in the dead air, darkness hanging close beyond the reach of Arol's light.

The other two came down quickly and Arol coded the canister to demagnetize the termination; it came slithering through the pipe, throwing distorted echoes around them.

Karmade was unable to catch his breath as they went on. He felt dizzy. He stumbled and almost fell, Lon grabbing him to keep him upright.

Lon and Arol exchanged a glance. Lon handed his blanket roll to Arol, unfolded something from his pocket, and strapped it over his shoulders; it looked like a big, flimsy papoose.

"I'll carry you," he said.

"Let me rest," Karmade said, waving him away. "Let me rest and I'll be OK." He started to lower himself down the curving wall.

"Josif," said Lon, and Josif took hold of Karmade and lifted him into the papoose. It took him a minute to strap it tight and for Lon to adjust it on his back, and then Karmade was riding piggyback in a confining sack that came almost to his shoulders, his legs dangling around Lon's waist. It was more humiliating than uncomfortable, and Karmade was too tired to complain.

They went on without a word. Now that Karmade wasn't walking there was no sound of footfalls.

After a while Arol whispered, "Stop."

"The end of the pipe is a hundred meters from us, by my stepcount," he murmured to Karmade. "Once we are out of the pipe you will no longer be shielded, so we may expect that the uppies' machines will begin sensing you. We are far enough from our encampments so that we are not afraid of the uppies, but for the sake of avoiding capture we will climb down into deep tunnels. We will be moving as quickly as we can, and silently, to evade both the uppies and the mutants who sometimes manage to slip through the Boundary Zone into these levels, and you must help us by holding on and staying quiet. Do you understand?"

"Just leave me here," Karmade said. "This is fine right here. I can make it the rest of the way myself."

Arol glanced at the other two. "Kaleth does not want the Old One to find you, and I promised her we would take you wherever you named before we returned," he said. "Now that we are away from the dwellings of our children, we are not afraid."

"What Arol means," said Lon ironically, "is now that we have disgraced ourselves by turning you out, we dare not disgrace ourselves further by abandoning you. You are a prisoner of our honor as much as we are ourselves. However, we do not wish to die for nothing. So you will cooperate with our efforts to save you so that we may forsake you to the mutants in accordance with our agreement with an old woman of our tribe. Is that a good summary, Arol?"

"Yes," said Arol, looking at him angrily. "So hold on and be quiet, upman, or we will tie and gag you. Let's go."

He turned and walked quickly, his light-patch dimmed so they could barely see the walls. In a minute he stopped again and crouched down. The magnetized termination from his canister made squeaking and crunching sounds as he ground it onto the floor even more firmly than last time. He tested it, then lowered himself over the edge a meter beyond, where the pipe suddenly stopped. Its dimly lit, jagged edges opening into black nothingness disappeared as his light dropped into the dark. Lon stepped forward to stand on the termination.

In a little while the harness came whizzing back up the cord. Lon put his foot in it and hit a key on the canister; it lowered him and Karmade rotating slowly through a space that could have been narrow or huge for all Karmade could tell. They went down maybe two hundred meters and then Karmade could see faint greenish light below, and soon Lon's free foot hit the ground. Arol pointed in a direction; Lon moved that way.

The harness whizzed upward behind them. A light-patch on Lon's jumpsuit glowed as he jogged through dank, moldy-smelling darkness. They were in the deep substructure of the old city upon which the City was built, Karmade guessed. A wall loomed out of the darkness, made of rough stone blocks that gleamed wetly in the light. Lon hesitated, then moved along it to the right. Twenty meters down a black tunnel opened. Lon carried Karmade a few meters into that, then stood still by the cold wall, turning off his light. Water dripped somewhere in the pitch-dark.

Lon's shoulders rose and fell as he breathed, still not very heavily. For Karmade the darkness was full of half-heard noises, half-seen shapes, as if his fever was coming back. A hissing had begun in his ears, not recognizable words but the lull of a voice, syllables.

A snap echoed outside the tunnel and a minute later a light came toward Lon and Karmade.

"OK," Arol breathed, Josif at his heels looking serious but excited. "Let's go."

They started to run then, an easy, loping jog that was surprisingly fast, rough stone floor visible for two meters ahead in Arol's light. From time to time Arol held a palm-sized map display in front of him. Occasionally he raised his hand and the men stopped and listened, holding their breath. They were almost as silent running as they were halted. Twice Arol led them into passages that opened off to the left.

*"Where are you?"* a hissing voice came suddenly clearly to Karmade. *"Call out."*

"What?"

*"I am here. Call out to me so I can find you in the dark."*

"No!"

Arol fell back two paces and hissed in Karmade's ear

as he ran: "Be quiet, upman! We don't know who may
be in these tunnels."

"*Call out. Call out,*" said the hissing voice. "*We are
very near to one another. I will take you. I will take you to
Her.*"

"No!" Karmade screamed in terror, and his voice
echoed with shocking, piercing volume through tunnels
that sounded like they went on forever. It was still running away through the dark, crashing into unseen walls,
when the Ur-men halted.

Arol's steely fingers forced Karmade's mouth open
and stuffed a rag into it, then tied a gag around the back
of his neck. Karmade's loudest scream now sounded like
a muffled grunt.

"Listen!" Lon hissed.

The other two froze.

A sound came from the darkness—a rustling, like
someone brushing against a wall nearby, or like many
running footsteps far off.

Arol's light went out and Karmade shook violently
on Lon's back, air roaring past his ears in the pitch-dark.

Arol's map—a sharp rectangle of light—blossomed
ahead of them for a second, and then Arol's light-patch
went on, very dimly. Karmade guessed there was a side
passage he didn't want to miss.

"*Come to me,*" the hissing voice said. "*I am here.*"

The tunnel curved gently to the left. Suddenly
around the curve two shiny spots came into view in the
dark.

The men slid to a stop, Josif falling on his rear. He
was up in a second and Arol was pulling one of the
blanket rolls from his shoulder.

The shape bulking behind the shiny eyes was huge
and humped; it began to move slowly forward with a
deep, guttural growling.

"*Come,*" it hissed in Karmade's head.

"Back up," said Arol, his voice hard and steady.

Lon scrambled backward, dragging Josif, leaving

Arol's silhouette leaning still and truculent against the vague moving shape.

Then the thing Arol had unwrapped from the blanket roll flashed with a rock-splitting bellow and the monstrous shape burst fire in a hundred places.

It screamed deafeningly and fell.

Arol's gesturing hand started Lon and Josif running again, dashing behind him past the huge shuddering body, hot blood spewing from smoking holes the autocannon had blown in it, and in that second Karmade saw that it was a man-shaped giant with no hair and very little face, cradling in its arms a tiny, blind, three-armed mutant.

The hissing voice in his head was screaming in agony.

Karmade lost consciousness.

When he woke he was jogging painfully on Lon's back again, but here the darkness had a noisome, filthy smell that made him want to hold his breath, and a vast booming like thunder shuddered the rocks of the tunnel. He tried to swallow and lick his lips, and choked on the rag in his mouth.

He coughed and struggled. Someone hissed an order and the men stopped running. Arol untied the gag and pulled the rag out.

Karmade tried to curse him but only a dry croaking would come. Josif held a water bottle to his lips and he gulped greedily. Arol's callused hand was pressed to his forehead.

"How do you feel?" Arol asked. "Can you keep yourself from screaming? You were unconscious for an hour and we were worried about you."

Karmade choked on the water and Josif took it away.

"The mutant—it was looking for me," he gasped, remembering. "It was calling me."

Arol eyed him curiously. "Well, I am not worried about the mutants," he said finally. "I am more worried about the uppies. I don't know what *that* is—" He gestured upward as the booming—which sounded like huge, distant explosions—shook dust and a few pebbles from the invisible ceiling. "I don't think it is for us, but it concerns me. We are near the Warren-Hole now; we need to hurry."

Karmade nodded. Josif helped him out of the papoose and walked him back and forth to get blood through his legs, gave him some more water and a strip of dried prototien to chew. Arol and Lon conferred in low voices a few meters away. Then he was strapped back in and they started off, the men running fast and eager, as if in a hurry to be done with their task. And with that perception, the terror of his situation came to Karmade full force.

But it was too late to change his mind.

They came to a heavy metal grating in a crumbling concrete wall. A foul smell came through it. Arol checked his map, then he and Josif yanked and pulled on the grating until it tumbled down with a ground-shaking boom that merged with the booming from above. Beyond, filthy water ran through a tunnel ten meters in diameter, a concrete walkway beside it. The men ran down the walkway.

Another concrete wall loomed in the dim light of Arol's patch, and the men stopped. There was another grating in front of them, this one much bigger and more sophisticated than the last: massively armored, mounted on enormous hinges, smart bolts holding it shut. The sewer flowed through its lower half.

"This is it," Arol said to Karmade over the booming from above as Lon unstrapped him from his back.

Karmade nodded. He couldn't talk. He was trembling violently.

"OK," said Arol uncomfortably as Lon steadied Karmade on his feet. "Well, I hope—I'm sorry—"

Lon peered into the impenetrable darkness beyond the grating. "You going in there?" he asked.

Karmade shrugged.

Lon studied him. "You have the bolt codes?"

Karmade shook his head, swallowing.

"You got a cloaker so the Maggots won't get you?"

Karmade shook his head again. He felt sick.

"Then how are you going to get down to the Warrens?"

"I—I don't know."

Lon and Arol looked at each other.

Then Arol grinned, and Lon's hard, lined, worried face cracked a little too, almost as if he was ashamed for anyone to see him smile.

"We're going to take him down to the Warrens," Arol told Josif. "Don't wait for us. Run back home. Run back and tell them we're honorable men."

"OK," said Josif, his young face shocked.

Lon and Arol yanked their blanket rolls into their hands and unwrapped their autocannons.

"Go on," Arol said patiently to Josif. Josif, staring into his face, backed into the darkness, and then, when they could barely see him anymore, turned and ran back the way they had come.

Arol nodded in satisfaction. He said to Karmade, "Step back."

Karmade stumbled numbly back against rock. Then a deafening boom crashed down from above, making the tunnel jump and dust and pebbles fall. The splitting bang of the cannons merged with it. A rock splinter hit Karmade painfully in the cheek, but through smoke and dust, almost opaque in Arol's light, he saw that the grating now hung ajar, the concrete along one side of it deeply cratered.

Lon dragged the grating open. Arol helped Karmade climb around its edge so he wouldn't fall into the stinking water that rushed obliviously into the darkness beyond.

"The uppies' blasting may have covered our entrance so that not every Maggot in a kilometer will converge on us," he murmured in Karmade's ear. "But now we must go fast."

As soon as they were in the tunnel beyond the grating Arol turned his light-patch up to full illumination. The light showed that the tunnel ended in a shaft, water flowing down steep spillways running back and forth along one stone wall, rusted metal stairs receding vertiginously down the other.

Arol pointed down the stairs.

They went down quickly and softly, Arol first, his cannon tracking back and forth against the darkness at the edges of his light, Lon behind turned almost backward, his light shining upward and his cannon jumping at shadows and chance gleams of water. They had gone down a hundred meters when Arol's cannon splintered the darkness. In the second before Lon's gun replied Karmade saw a metal slug with four rotating heads explode in flames swallowed by black smoke; then proton lightning burned into his eyes the image of Lon spitted on a fork of blinding blue and another Maggot tumbling in flames through the shaft between water and stairs. Fragments of it sent up geysers of steam from the spillway. Arol pulled Karmade down the stairs faster than Lon's smoking body fell. Then they were at the bottom, at a dead end where the spillway water rushed through another massive grating into darkness.

Arol threw Karmade into that water.

It was deep. His feet smashed into the grating, legs buckling, the rushing water crushing him against it with bone-breaking force. There was a blinding, jarring explosion and the metal swung away in front of him. The water yanked and tumbled him over and over into darkness slashed with afterimages of fire and a last glimpse of Arol crouching, autocannon blazing, hair flying around his head.

# 12

Karmade floated in absolute darkness.

He felt calm somehow, though he knew he was in the Warrens. Buoyed by the foam-insulated jumpsuit the Ur-people had given him, he floated with a gentle current that no longer felt cold, whose smell no longer registered in his nostrils, listening to the vast, faraway explosions that shivered the water and rock around him like distant thunder.

He thought he knew what they were: the beginning of the City's operation to "sterilize" the underground land. He felt sure now that Nelda Cloud's people had orchestrated the phony mutant breakout explosions to goad the City into this, the unknowing destruction of the only beings—humans, mutants, aliens, or whatever they were—who could threaten her absolute control of ZantCorp. It would mean enormous slaughter; estimates put the population of the underground sheltercity in the hundreds of thousands.

And all to keep a cycling hyperdopaminergic antiager free to indulge in delusional ritual murders.

The only saving grace, thought Karmade, was that he would probably be out of the whole mess before too long.

The water was slow and quiet, the darkness impenetrable, but after a while a patch of afterimage came back, or perhaps it was a trick of the eyes from such a long time of looking at nothing, or perhaps—

The patch, a dull splotch of orange, grew so slowly that Karmade was still in doubt when it was a hundred meters away and he could faintly see the outline of a broken doorway.

But as he came closer down the black river and heard the water lapping monotonously at the jetty below the door, there could be no doubt that he had come to an inhabited, or at least an illuminated, region.

He swam four strokes from the middle of the channel to the concrete lip of the underground land and pulled himself up out of the water, the ancient concrete crumbling under his hands, its pebbles hurting his knees. He stood, jumpsuit dripping, looking through a doorway in a wall that had been poured more than a hundred years ago during the frantic preparations for the biowars.

The faint orange light—which would have been invisible to anyone whose eyes weren't used to absolute darkness—showed a short passage, rubble of its decomposition covering the floor, and at the end of that another shapeless doorway the light came through a little more strongly.

A vast explosion from above made the ground hum under Karmade's feet, and a few pebbles fell from the walls and ceiling of the passage.

He walked forward slowly, feet crunching on rubble. A handful of loose concrete fell from the doorsill as he steadied himself against it, bringing the harsh, dry smell of cement dust through what he suddenly realized was the pervading stink of the sewer.

He crouched down against the passage wall to rest

and think. Maybe he could hide here from the mutants and ZantCorp. But there was no food here, or drinkable water, and he suddenly realized he was hungry and thirsty.

He stood up and limped down the passage toward the light.

There were rubbled rooms, some of the walls collapsed, corroded airlock doors fallen or leaning on their hinges, everything filled with a dead stillness that the distant booming lay upon like an uneasy dream. Karmade's jumpsuit was soon covered with a grey coat of dust as he walked through what he guessed had been a military barracks. He followed the orange light until he found that it came from an old, jagged lumtile fragment cemented into the wall of a room a hundred meters from the underground river. The tile had been put there much more recently than the war, he judged, but it lit only decay, throwing eerie shadows in the rubble.

He walked through a low concrete cavern off the room with the lumtile, then through other rooms. As soon as the light had faded almost to nothing behind him he thought he saw another light ahead. He picked his way toward it and it was another lumtile fragment, a long sliver cemented onto a doorsill so that it lit a room and a passage, as if whoever had put it there was trying to make maximum use of its light. There was a third light too, in the wall of a passage farther on.

Someone had traced a dim path through the ruins of these barracks to the underground river, for what purpose he couldn't guess. But it suggested this place wasn't always deserted.

Then he heard the singing.

It came from a long way off, falling dead in the dusty ruins, so that when it stopped he thought he had imagined it, imagined something so lovely in this dead place.

But it came again, high and clear though faint and faraway, singing a haunting music.

He stood frozen, fear, wonder, desire, and hunger

circling through his mind. Finally, slowly, he started toward the sound.

It came through pitch-dark passages that he groped and stumbled along; a few times he thought small things scuttled away from his feet. Finally a faint light came from ahead and he went faster, picking his way through the rubble. The voice was singing words he understood.

The light got brighter and at every doorway and turn he expected to see what was making it, but he went on until he was almost blinded, until he came at last to a doorway with *plants* growing through it—branches with big, lush leaves, vines creeping along the rubble, even a small, sickly flower.

He stared in astonishment. Light glared through the foliage and there was a tinkle of water, and the voice sang again, very near:

> *"When I see the upper air,*
> *And when the sun shines down on me,*
> *When the clouds go sailing high,*
> *Then in the land of life I'll be."*

Karmade silently pushed leaves aside and looked between them.

It was a little grotto in a sunny garden where bushes and small trees grew. A tiny, clear stream tinkled down the rough stone of a wall that vines climbed. The air was faintly perfumed by flowers. He could feel the heat of the sun burning down.

A slender, naked girl stood with her back to him, pale hair in a thin braid. She stood by a small pool the stream tinkled into, dipping the toes of one foot into the water rhythmically as she hummed to herself. Then she raised her clear, beautiful voice again:

> *"Though that grass be fresh and green,*
> *And though that air be tempting sweet,*
> *Not a one of these things I'll see,*
> *Until my soul the Taker meet."*

A breeze stirred the leaves around her. She knelt by the pool and, still humming, began to splash water onto her face and shoulders.

Karmade pushed carefully through the leaves and branches and stood two meters behind her, filled with awkwardness and shame.

"Excuse me," he said, his voice clumsy and hoarse. It was the only thing he could think of to say. The girl whirled and stood in a quick, light motion, and a few drops of the water from her hands splashed on him.

He took a step backward then, heart pounding, because she was a mutant, slitted blue eyes ogling blindly in the direction of his voice, and at the same time he saw that the place she stood in was a primitive counterfeit of the sunny garden he had first taken it for. The "sunlight" came from hundreds of lumtile fragments of different shapes, sizes, and tints cemented in an uneven surface over a low ceiling and giving off a sickly glare; the heat was supplied by rusty coils mounted over the lumtiles. The breeze that had rustled the leaves came from a fan set on a shelf in the sloping concrete wall, and the stream came from a pipe near its top. The one real thing about the place was the plants, obviously mutants, with monstrous, fleshy leaves and strange tassels, growing spindly and sickly out of patches of composted garbage, but their few small flowers giving off a delicate, intoxicating smell.

"You should not be here," said the girl in a soft, even voice, searching for him with her blind eyes. "This is my day. You will have yours sometime, if you have not already. Go and leave me alone."

Looking up he saw that someone had painted a crude mural on the concrete wall behind her—a blue field, and on it a yellow ball with rays coming out, and several convex white blobs—the sun and clouds.

"Go and leave me alone," said the girl again. He saw then that she was not beautiful, as her voice had made him think. She was bone-thin and the stigmata of malnutrition were on her: face deeply lined though she seemed to be only in her teens, ribs sticking out under skinny, sagging breasts, hands already gnarled at some backbreaking work, long legs bent inward with rickets.

Even as he dropped his eyes in shame, his voice was saying: "I'm hungry. Do you have any food? Could I drink some of your water?"

"Who are you?" As he hesitated she went on: "Of course I have some food. They give you extra on your day. Don't you know? Look, I'll share some with you if you are really hungry. But then you must go away."

She knelt and took a little bundle from under a scraggly bush by the pool. She unwrapped it and stood again, holding it out to him. He stepped forward timidly; there was something about her that made him feel unclean. The bundle was full of chunks of prototien, scraps and rinds, the kind you would throw away after a meal in the City, throw into the garbage chute to the building compactor for eventual disposal into the Warrens.

He crammed them ravenously into his mouth, barely noticing that some of them were moldy. He tried to stop before they were all gone, to leave some for the starved girl, but he could not. But she didn't seem to mind; she smiled a little as he finished, dusting the crumbs into his palm and funneling them into his mouth.

"You *are* hungry. Everyone is hungry these days."

He knelt and put his face into the stream, drank the brackish, poison-tasting water as if it were ambrosia. As he finished, the dull booming above them, which had been going on almost without a break, momentarily got louder.

He jumped up in panic. "They're coming!"

The girl's face twisted with the sudden fear of a child, then smoothed out again. She raised her blind eyes toward the ceiling. "Soon," she whispered.

"Will you leave now?" she said softly in another minute. "If I am lucky enough for my day to come up just before the end of everything, you wouldn't interfere with that, would you?"

"I—I can't leave."

"Who are you?" she whispered, as if knowing suddenly that was the question that needed answering.

"I—I'm from—up there," he choked.

She took a step backward, afraid again. "A godie? Are—are you going to kill me?"

"No."

She stood still for a minute, staring as if trying to penetrate her blindness. Then she dropped to her knees. "They say sometimes angels visit people in the garden on their day—" she whispered in awe.

"I'm not an angel."

"Then why are you here?"

"I'm—people want to kill me up there. I had to go somewhere."

"Tell me," she breathed, "about Up There. Is it very beautiful? All we have is stories and the words of those who are sent down to us, but they usually will not talk to us, and die soon anyway of sickness or sadness. It is my day, and I would dearly love to hear—just once—"

" 'Your day—' "

"Yes. There is a lottery. Once in everyone's life they have a day when they can go into one of the gardens alone, and know what it is like to live real Life, instead of what we have now. The gardens are too small and precious to let everyone in all the time—they would be trampled and ruined. They give you as much food as you want and you don't have to work. They tell you, 'Pay attention and remember. You will have this day to remember your whole life.' "

The booming came again, very loud, as if the explosions, the systematic excavation to bare the Warrens to the City's soldiers, were getting nearer. A few pebbles rattled to the concrete floor.

"They're coming," Karmade rasped. "Don't you know they're coming?"

"Yes."

"And you don't care if you die?"

"Why should I care?"

He looked down at her, at her clear, blind eyes and calm, upturned face.

In a minute she asked him again, "Is it very beautiful Above? Can you see the sky? Are there gardens as beautiful as this one? I would dearly love to hear . . ."

He stared at her lined cheeks and hunger-ravaged body, at the stigmata of her twisted DNA as the bombs boomed dully above and the little stream tinkled into the crudely hollowed pool in the concrete floor. Then he lowered himself next to her and began to talk. He told her of the gardens in Sentrex, of the flowering trees arching over little bowers where you could drowse all day listening to the humming of bees, smelling the sweet perfume of flowers, the deep crystalline blue of the sky full of the sun's glare, and of the moon, and the flowering ponds he had washed in, and of the stars. She listened at first with rapturously parted lips, blind eyes fixed on his face, but then by degrees her head bowed and leaned against him until, when he got up gently, she was fast asleep, her bone-thin shoulder rising and falling with her breathing as she lay curled on the concrete floor.

He walked through the tattered little garden. It was long and narrow, as if landscaped inside one of the barrack rooms. At the end was a metal door of the kind he had seen in the ruins, but this one fixed firmly in its frame and fastened shut with a pressure lock.

He hesitated, then turned the lock wheel.

The door hissed slightly opening, and a smell came through—the smell of the Warrens, he realized. He trembled and almost locked the door again.

But there was no use trying to hide or torturing the girl anymore.

He pushed the door ponderously open.

The smell came strong about him, a stink of human grime, food, excreta, sweat, ancientness. The girl behind him moaned in her sleep, as if the smell brought bad dreams.

He went out quickly and pushed the door shut. It locked with a click.

He was in a dim, narrow street with an arched ceiling. At the end of the street a dark, hooded figure stood.

It came toward him. His heart pounded and he stepped backward against the metal door. The mutants ate normals that happened into the Warrens, they said, even ate each other in their savagery and starvation.

The figure was wrapped in dark, tattered robes. As it came near it put back its hood.

It was a man. Thin and stooped, deeply lined face a sickly grey, but a man nevertheless, without deformities or stigmata that Karmade could see. His pale grey eyes studied Karmade.

Finally he said in a low, rasping voice, "So you have come. But too late."

Karmade stood fearful and bewildered, clutching the handle of the metal door. "What do you mean? Who do —who do you think I am?"

"Theodore Karmade. Theodore Karmade, who has come too late to save us from the destruction he has brought upon us." He raised a withered hand to indicate the booming above, now almost painful in its shuddering intensity. "If you had either stayed out of matters entirely or come down here sooner, things might have been different."

"Are you a . . . a . . . ." Karmade quavered.

"Telepath, yes. But not a Speaker, only a Listener, and a very poor one at that—I cannot listen through the hubbub in the upland, for instance. I could only distinguish your voice once you were alone in the water of our land, and then I knew you were coming to us. But hurry. Hurry now and we may yet live, and thousands of others may live, though I cannot see how. Though if you are here it means you escaped from ZantCorp somehow, and that gives me hope; perhaps the Watchers are influencing events after all. So let us hurry; there may still be time."

He turned and started quickly back up the narrow street.

Karmade stood frozen with fear and disorientation.

The man stopped and looked back at him. "Do you want to die, godie? Hurry!"

Karmade lurched toward him fearfully. "Will we— are there mutants around here?" he blurted before he realized his blunder.

"Yes," said the man. "Thousands of them."

They came out of the narrow street and the mutants were all around them.

There was a wider street out there, its concrete ceiling high, and along both sides of it dark holes opening at ground level and higher up, which had once been the doors and windows of the shelter-city but which were now just crumbling concrete caves like ancient tombs. The walls at street level were worn smooth and darkened with the grime of bodies passing over many years. Cracked antique lumtiles gave off a greyish light.

It was full of people in cast-off clothes and rags, a few naked, some carrying bundles, all hurrying down the steeply sloping, curving street, the scuffling of their feet sounding between the ground-shaking explosions.

There were few whose mutations were great enough to be obvious, Karmade saw. A little girl in a ragged dress looked up at him as she passed from a serious, lined face, eyes full of dark thought; she was pulled along by an old, old woman without teeth, eyes almost hidden by folds of skin, who seemed feebleminded: she cackled and nodded to herself as she hobbled along as fast as she could with the ragged crowd. A man whose legs and arms seemed to bend the wrong way, like a dog's, crept hunched over and leaning on two rough crutches, staring at the ground with his sweating, dead-white face.

A grotesquely huge fat man with giant earlobes and an enormously wide face stood naked in the middle of the street and began to wail and blubber, his eyes rolling while his huge hands opened and closed spasmodically.

The black-robed man who was leading Karmade began pushing through the crowd toward him.

Karmade hesitated, dizzy and nauseated, terrified of touching the mutants. *But they're humans,* he realized, looking at them. *People.* He followed the man, brushing bad-smelling shapes he tried to keep from seeing.

The black-robed man stopped by the bellowing giant, who was a full meter taller and looked two hundred kilograms heavier.

"Man," he said. "Man! Do you hear me?"

The huge man looked down, earlobes flopping. "Y-yes," he blubbered.

"Do you remember what you are supposed to do? You are going down to the deep parts with all the other people, to save yourself. Do you remember?"

"Y-yes."

"You must hurry and save yourself. You must not stop or be afraid. Do you remember?"

"Y-yes."

"Then go. Hurry. *Hurry.*" And he gave the huge man a sharp slap on his hip. The man turned ponderously, still sobbing, and began lumbering along with the crowd, his footfalls palpable through the concrete.

A roar from above shook pebbles and dust from the ceiling.

There were screams, and a surge of the crowd almost knocked Karmade down. He yelled with fright, his voice blending with the others.

A hand closed on his arm. "Don't worry," the black-robed man's voice said in his ear. "It's only death; nothing to fear."

They went with the crowd, Karmade with his eyes half closed, head bowed so as to see as little as possible. The man led him surely and quickly, pausing now and then to help someone or give words of encouragement. At intervals in the street voices yelled for the crowd to keep moving.

The street kept sloping downward and curving around so that you could only see about thirty meters

ahead. Karmade knew the shelter-city had been built in
descending spirals, with the high-isolation areas at the
bottom. And not all the people in the shelters had been
able to get into the high-iso areas during the extremity
of the biowar, so that when the surface populations had
died outright from the mutagenic retrovirus plagues and
the VIPs in the high-iso areas had been protected, those
left on these spiral streets had been infected just enough
so that many of their descendants had become mutants,
who had now lived here a hundred years—

The explosions had become a little less deafening as
they went downward, and now the street came out into
a circular open space perhaps 250 meters across.
Karmade could see other openings along the walls where
other streets ended, and people hurrying out of them,
thousands of people heading toward a five-meter hole in
the ground at the very center of the open space, the
crowd crushing downward along what looked like spiral
stairs set into its walls. A few figures seemed to be di-
recting, urging the crowd into the hole, trying to keep
order. But not everyone was going into the hole.

Near the hole was an enormous concrete cube, ten
meters on a side. Hundreds of the people jamming the
big circular space were milling around it, pressing forward to touch it, kneeling by it.

The black-robed man cursed quietly. He pulled
Karmade in that direction, hand tight on his arm. As
they came to the dense and chaotic crowd by the cube,
with all around them the hiss of breath and smell of
panic, the man began to yell over the hubbub of voices.

"Get up! Get up! There is no time! *They* cannot help
us if we don't help ourselves! The fire from Above is
coming! Get into the shaft and *then* pray! Hurry now!
Get up! Get up!"

His voice was mostly drowned by the confusion but
the figures nearest began to pay attention, looking
around first with surprise and then sheepish respect, as if
he were a prominent person. A few got up and began to
push desperately toward the central shaft as if they had

suddenly remembered their danger. Others followed, and then, as he continued to yell, there was a sudden stampede.

Karmade could barely hear the man's voice as sweating flesh and hard bone slammed against him and a hand clawed his chest. He fought desperately to stay on his feet.

An enormous explosion in one of the streets opening on the central space sent dust and smoke billowing into the air; the crowd screamed and the stampede toward the high-iso shaft became a tidal wave.

A strong hand pulled Karmade backward. He fought stinking bodies, arms, legs, hands. Then the black-robed man had him in the lee of the giant concrete cube, the struggling mutants pushing toward the shaft jostling but no longer crushing them. The man was gasping for breath and his face was bloody. He seemed to be in shock.

"Too late. Too late," Karmade saw rather than heard his bloody lips murmuring. He turned his face away and took something from his torn robes, moved it in front of the concrete cube's surface.

A hole in that surface reached out and swallowed them.

# 13

The hole in the cube closed and the noise of the crowd and explosions was cut off; there was sudden dead silence that made Karmade's ears ring.

His breath and the black-robed mutant's breath gasped in the dead air of a pitch-black space that could have been tiny or big. A small area of dim illumination, shining down on a smooth black floor, surrounded them. Karmade saw that it came from the thing the man had moved in front of the outside wall to open the hole: a softly glowing cube of flawless crystal.

The mutant stared into Karmade's face, the light throwing his eyes and sunken cheeks into shadow. "Listen to me, godie; listen while I try to tell you enough so that you—but it is *too late.*" He sobbed. The blood on his face was coming from one of his eyes, Karmade saw, and his lips trembled with injury and exhaustion and the need to speak quickly. "But perhaps we can still save something. *Listen.*" He took hold of Karmade's arms with trembling hands. "There are other beings besides humans living in the solar system. No, don't waste time being surprised. They conceal themselves from us, though for reasons no one understands they take an interest in us. Until the mutations came that allowed some of our people to listen to thoughts, even thoughts beyond the Earth, there was no way we could have detected them. But that is another story, and there is no time.

"These beings swim in the darkness between the planets on fields of energy. Yet they cannot come near our planet, the Listeners say, because of a field of poison or darkness that hangs around it. None had come to Earth for millennia when Nova and Irneldo Zant happened upon some near the planet Neptune.

"But they desired to come, I believe; for some reason the exocreatures desired to come to Earth, perhaps to try to help mankind, whose insanity and suffering they had watched for so long. In Nova and Irneldo they saw an opportunity to slip through the field of darkness. They *coupled* with them and sent them back to Earth penetrated with their seed—not pregnant, but penetrated with the patterns of their growth so that as time went on the creatures grew in them, making them hybrid beings, and when they had their daughter she too had the pattern—"

He coughed a fine spray of blood.

"After some years Nova and Irneldo came to the stage where their physical appearance began to change, and they knew they couldn't hide from the godies who hunt for mutants in your precious, pure City. By this time they knew that the same change would happen in time to their baby daughter, but that it would take years. So they modified her psychoneural functioning as well as they could to allow the creature to grow in her without too much pain and without attracting too much attention—and conditioned her against sex, which could destructively accelerate the awakening of the exocreature—and they came secretly down through the Boundary Zone to us—to me."

His grey eyes were dim now, and his grey, wrinkled face looked very old.

"I remember how afraid they were when they first came, though they had food and huge invisible machines with them, and androids and weapons. As if we might eat them; as if just the sight of us might kill them. They were suffering greatly with their form transition. They asked if they could stay with us, and we in the council told them we accepted everyone, turned no one away—because of course there is nowhere else to go.

"Their machines built this place." He waved his hand at the darkness around them. "It was disguised on the outside as a concrete worship-structure to fool any remote sensors the godies might send down—though it is against their great laws to do that, since it might give someone occasion to pity us.

"I was assigned by the council to watch over the Zants, to trade our help and knowledge and goodwill for as much food and medicine as we could get. We sent them the few of our people whose mutations had caused them to change shape radically at some time—but even these came back shocked at what they saw in the hidden chambers where the man and woman lay. Soon the androids and machines would let no one come near them, though the work of building their enclosure went on and on until we surmised that it must be of mighty size, though all contained somehow within this cube. But we didn't have the luxury of speculating too long, because our lives were devoured, as they always have been, with the impossible task of keeping our people alive, keeping the garbage food sorting and distribution networks running, quarantining and caring for the sick, watching over those too deviated to care for themselves, and trying always to teach the children a little, just enough so that they remain human, do not forget they are human.

"Still, I remember well the last time I talked to the Zants. I was wakened by one of their androids. It told me the man Irneldo had to speak with me right away and that he could not wait even an hour—this was the end, they were vanishing as humans.

"I hurried to the cube with the android, sat at the communication station they had set up for me. Irneldo's words came through a speech synthesizer, as though he could no longer even talk understandably, and there were long pauses at times.

" 'My friend, we are elapsing,' said the synthesizer. 'We thank you for the help you have given us and wish you success in your struggles.' This although we had traded for everything we had given them, and driven hard bargains. 'I have no time for fine words or to prepare you for what I am going to say. I find that I must beg you for one more favor. I wish to leave my daughter in your care.' "

"I was astonished but tried to stay composed. My mind was racing to calculate what I might ask in barter for such a duty. I was mindful of the council's instructions to take every possible advantage of these fabulously rich people.

" 'The AI systems watching over her are as sophisticated as we could build,' the synthesizer went on, 'but no machine can address every circumstance. The systems annunciate into our tomb'—he had the habit of calling this structure a tomb—'and if you accept my charge I will ask that you monitor them to ensure that our daughter is protected. An extensive training course has been programmed for you—of course, you will have to abandon your other duties.'

" 'I am eager to help you,' I told the communication station. 'But how could my people be compensated for the loss of my services? I am one of the few who was educated Above before my deviation expressed itself, and so can scarcely be spared.'

" 'You are a tireless servant of your people,' the machine said flatly. The pauses were becoming longer now, as if Irneldo was fading farther and farther away. 'I have no time to bargain with you, nor the strength, but I tell you that if you do this for us . . . and do it faithfully, so

that our automation brings our beloved . . . . daughter
safe to us after her term of years Above, . . . . . . I
tell you that when she comes . . . into our tomb and
wakes us . . . . . . . . . I make a solemn . . . . . . . .
vow       that      . . .      we      . . . . . . . .      will
. . . . . . . . . . . . . . .      fulfill      your      age-long
. . . . . . . . . . . ,'

"I hammered and screamed at the machine until my
throat was raw and my hands bloody, but Irneldo would
not come back; he was gone.

"Upon hearing my report, the council agreed that
Irneldo Zant had intended to promise us something of
great importance, and agreed to give me up to the task
he had asked me to do. Though no one would say it
aloud, all of us hoped the creatures the man and woman
had become could somehow deliver us from our impris-
onment under the ground.

"The machines that watched over the Zant girl were
of the utmost complexity and it took me hard study to
master them, but soon I was following her movements
every day, monitoring the protective systems, making
sure they carried out their functions. Because I was the
only one who could get into this cube, and because
the rumor had gone around our city like wildfire that the
godie man and woman would return to bring us out of
our bondage, I became the high priest of a new religion
conceived in the minds of our tormented people. I was
now a person of superstition among them. And in secret
I earned my reputation; I made adjustments and deci-
sion overrides that saved the Zant girl from danger several times. The main danger now came from her aunt
the madwoman, because the one thing Irneldo and
Nova Zant had not foreseen with their exocreature-
enhanced genius was that Nelda Cloud would suffer
central nervous system damage as a result of the anti-
aging treatments she began to take after they died, and
would become a paranoid schizophrenic always plotting
against her niece . . .

"But I am rambling as my people die," he said, his

face twisting with shock and remembrance. He began to breathe hard, until Karmade was afraid his heart would fail. "As time went on the growth of the exocreature in her made the girl unstable despite—or perhaps because of—the personality modifications her parents had performed; she began to remember just enough about them to become obsessed with finding them. Then her security people hired you to foil a suicide attempt—which I myself was working to stop—and the girl used you to escape from their custody and from my machines' surveillance. That was the worst day of my life, even worse than the day I was thrown into the Warrens, because I knew that if I had lost her our people had lost their hope of rescue. And it was scarcely better when I found that her sexual contact with you and your reequilibration therapy had begun to disturb the exocreature in her, awaken it too fast. I knew that within weeks her body would start showing signs of the change, and then the godies would seize her—

"The Zants' AI systems were crammed with contingency plans for such a circumstance, and clones had been growing for years to replace her in the event that she had to be taken suddenly. As soon as I saw there was no alternative, I mobilized the hypercloaked modules the Zants had left in Sentrex—invisible even to Quasar's cloaking belts—and watched for an opportunity to take her and make it look like she had died. This was so the godie authorities and her aunt would not suspect what had happened, would not come down here looking for her, discover our secret, perhaps destroy Nova and Irneldo as they slept.

"For that is what the exo/human creatures were doing deep in this cube fortress, their 'tomb'—sleeping. I am a Listener of a poor sort but I soon learned not to listen too closely to the deep insides of the cube—areas forbidden to me by the Zants in any case—and sense the strange, terrible dreams forming there.

"So we brought Quasar Zant, sedated, down into the underground world. Her parents had wished her to live as a human on the surface as long as possible, away from the horrors of this place, but now that was at an end. Of course she was terrified when she awoke, and even more terrified when I told her about her parents in a clumsy attempt to console her, but soon she passed beyond our power to help. The transformation you had artificially accelerated had twisted her mind. I tried to explain that she would have to stay with us until her change had progressed far enough for her to know how to wake her parents, but she didn't seem to hear or understand.

"And then my plans began to fall apart. Because instead of being prosecuted for the girl's death you escaped from Sentrex, and the cloaking belts Zant security recovered from you and Quasar led them to discover information that Nelda Cloud realized meant her sister and brother-in-law might be alive in the Warrens. She began to fear that they might return to claim the wealth she planned to use to keep herself eternally young."

"But—you *helped* me escape from Sentrex," Karmade blurted. He was dazed, trying to follow the old man's story, concentrating to understand it. "The voice in my head—mutant telepathy—"

The mutant was silent suddenly, staring at Karmade with his bloody, shadowed eyes.

"You told me to get in the bag," Karmade stuttered. "You—"

The mutant's voice shook. "A voice led you out of Sentrex?"

"It—made me resist their hypnointerrogation—not tell about the Warren-Hole—and then—and then it told me how to escape, get in the bag—"

"What did it sound like?"

"Whispering. Hissing."

The old man's eyes closed and his chin sagged onto his chest. After a minute he nodded slowly and looked up. "So that is how it happened," he said.

"There arose a faction in the council with followers among our people," he went on after another pause, "that insisted we should not wait for the girl to live out her time on the surface, but bring her here right away, kidnap her if necessary, get her to wake her parents so they could deliver us from our bondage. Every day for us here is a day of desperation, hunger, despair. Some of the faction's followers formed a sect in the 'religion' of the cube—poor, maddened souls who could not wait and watch their children starve, watch them turn into mindless, snuffling things rooting for scraps of food in the streets. They had no idea that the machines I controlled from inside the cube could bring the girl to us anytime—Irneldo had wisely prohibited the council from telling anyone about the details of my work.

"I thought it was better—I *knew* it was better that we should keep our side of the bargain to the letter, no matter how the people clamored—that we should leave the girl on the surface until it was her time to come down, just as her parents wished.

"But one of the most prominent of the Accelerators, as this faction called itself, was a brilliant, young, highly deviated telepath, who at times, I suspect, and against the express decisions of the council, spoke to Quasar Zant in her building on the surface. He was a powerful Speaker as well as a consummate Listener; so consummate that he swore he could hear the Ones who had penetrated the Zants, whom he believed sit at great distances and watch the Earth, and whom I have thought I have heard in snatches sometimes, their voices too faint and sweet to really believe in. But he said they sang songs of deliverance, that they could not come to us because of the cloud of evil that hangs over our planet, but that they were determined to find a way—"

"He was tiny and blind," Karmade said slowly. "He had three arms, and a giant carried him—"

"How do you know?" snapped the mutant, his eyes wide. "How do you know that?"

"We saw him—in the tunnel—Death-Hole Warren. He—she seemed to know he would be there—his guards tried to grab her. I—"

"The girl? In the Warrens? When?"

"When she escaped from the 'drome—the Dusk House, she took me to the Warren-Hole and— She said his voice spoke to her in her head— Then we met him in a tunnel above the Boundary Zone, looking for me, and —the sewer tribesmen who brought me—killed him—"

The mutant's face stopped him.

"So that is how it happened," the mutant gasped finally. "So we have only ourselves to blame for our doom. Solen spoke to the girl, telling her he knew where her parents were. She went to meet him in the upshaft— all the rest happened as a result. Then Solen kept you from telling ZantCorp about us, helped you escape from Sentrex, tried to bring you down here so you could continue the girl's awakening, so she could wake her parents, deliver us from our torment. And thus Nelda Cloud found out that the Zants were alive, and she arranged the explosions and political hysteria to goad the godies into destroying us— Yes. Yes. It makes sense. It is all in the balance of things, action and reaction, sowing and reaping, cause and effect. The river of souls flows in perfect symmetry over the long run, over the long run—"

He was babbling incoherently now, fists clenching and unclenching as if he had become unhinged, blood trickling from around his eye again, but he suddenly cut off short and blurted: "Godie, you are the only one who can help us now. And you will do it. I vow that *you will do it*, as penance for your people's torture of us. Do you understand?" He grabbed Karmade and shook him violently. "Do you understand?" Karmade pushed him off, backed away from his maddened glare.

The mutant began to tremble. He wiped a sleeve over his bloody, sweating face. "We have no hope now," he mumbled. "No hope! After everything, all our suffering, we have nothing but death. Unless we can wake the beings now. Unless you can wake the creature in the girl that knows how to wake the beings—for she herself does not know how. She is here, in this cube, in a special chamber, sedated—"

"Get someone else," Karmade quavered, backing away into the blank darkness. "I can't. I just want to—to—"

"To die? You are going to die with the rest of us if you do nothing. Unless they wake up—and perhaps even if they wake up—you are going to die, godie. Do you understand?

"We have no one with your training down here, nor anyone with your brain-wave affinity with the girl. Contact with you and your psychomanipulation nearly woke her before. No one but you can do it. It may kill her—or you—to wake the creature so quickly—but *you must try*—!"

Quasar lay on a bare mattress in a room of grey stone blocks fit together so perfectly the seams barely showed, ragged blankets pulled up to her shoulders, her hair tangled with sweat. The room was lit from nowhere, and part of one wall appeared to be a rectangular mirror. The air smelled of her heavy sleep. Karmade stood over her holding the "key" the mutant had given him, the cube of crystal that had glowed softly in the pitch-dark outside the room, showing the perfect 2-D mirror that was its "door."

He was alone with her. After leading him to the mirror door, the mutant had taken him to the outer wall again and shown him how to move the cube in a loop-over-cross motion to create an opening. With a sudden shock of light, intense roaring, and a flash of figures running through smoke, the wall sucked the mutant outside and abruptly shut again, returning the darkness and silence. In near panic Karmade had run back to the mirror and moved the cube loop-over-cross. The mirror had turned inside out and Karmade was in the room with Quasar.

He knelt and looked at her face. It was pale and tense, but she didn't look injured. Even unconscious she seemed to Karmade more alive than anyone he had ever seen. She lay on her side; he rolled her a little to peel a sedative patch off her neck, noticing that the silastic catheters to her carotids had been taped over to prevent infection. Then he sat back to watch her wake up and think about what he was supposed to do when she did.

Reintegrate her personality around the exocreature complex the mutant claimed was in her, then get her to remember something she had never learned: how to "wake up" two creatures that had once been her parents and that the mutant claimed were somewhere in this enclosure too. And all this without neurointerventive technology, and within the few hours it would take the City to transport nuclear explosives to the superhardened high-iso enclosure where the mutants were hiding. Very simple. And impossible.

The girl swallowed and brushed a clumsy, sleeping hand across her face, then rolled into a more comfortable position. In a few minutes her eyebrows knitted and she swallowed again thirstily. Karmade was the first thing she saw when she opened her eyes.

She studied him, closed her eyes again, then opened them. Then she got up on her elbow, face filling with confusion and fear.

"Where—where am I?" she croaked. "What time is it? Where am I?"

"I don't know what time it is," he said. "You're in the Warrens."

Panic flared in her eyes, and she started to shake. She lay back down, staring at the ceiling.

"I'm thirsty," she said after a while, eyes flickering at him.

There was a faintly foul-smelling sanitary module in the corner, with a water dispenser and disposable cups. He brought her four cups before her thirst was slaked. Then she lay back again dully.

"What are you going to do with me?" she asked. He couldn't tell whether she remembered him or not.

"Try to get you to remember some things."

"Like the other one." She shivered. "He's horrible. You better let me go, you understand? If my aunt catches you, you'll be worse off than dead."

Karmade's heart sank. "What do you remember about your aunt?"

"She takes care of me. She's my guardian. And if you hurt me, she'll hurt you. Worse than hurt you."

She had regressed to her infantile/dependent personality, he saw, which actually regarded her aunt as a protector. The impossibility of what he had to do struck Karmade with renewed force. It would take multiple sessions on the CNS-HED to get her even to remember who he was, he guessed, much less effect a reintegration of her personalities.

He sat down against the wall and closed his eyes. Might as well just wait here for the nuclear explosions that would vaporize this structure along with the rest of the Warrens.

Quasar had curled up fetally in her blankets and was sucking her thumb, looking at him from dull eyes.

He had an idea then, a vague, idle idea.

"Quasar," he said, and his voice was soft and vague and idle. "Listen to me. Just relax and listen. Listen to my voice. Don't worry about remembering anything; don't worry about anything. Just relax and listen. You can close your eyes if it feels more comfortable, and if it helps you to listen to my voice. That's it. Close your eyes. My voice is very relaxing, very soothing.

"That's it. You feel relaxed, very relaxed. Your muscles are relaxing. You can feel them relaxing. You feel heavy, very heavy and relaxed. Your toes are feeling nice and warm and very relaxed. Now the relaxation is spreading from your toes to your feet. You're safe here with me, safe and warm and relaxed. Now the warmth and relaxation is spreading to your ankles. They're heavy as lead, so relaxed you just don't want to move them, you just want to lie there and feel them, feel your warm, relaxed feet, so heavy you can't move them . . ."

He went through the hypnotic induction procedure

slowly and languidly, half going into a trance himself, not really caring if it worked or not. It didn't matter one way or the other. It would have been a long shot at the best of times, and even the best MPD hypnotherapy took months to show results, but it was something to pass the time, something that might have been useful if he had started it long ago. What had put the idea in his head was the recollection that infantile/dependent personalities were strongly susceptible hypnotic subjects.

He languidly gave her the works, counting backward, having her listen to waves on a warm, sunny beach, sending her down, down, down in an elevator, and all the rest of it, the whole procedure that was done automatically by the psych-booth expert systems he had supervised as a Guild psych tech, long ago, in another lifetime.

At the end of it she lay completely still, barely breathing, the statue of a sleeping woman. Karmade had been careful all along to suggest that she could still hear his voice, and now he gave her some suggestions to rate her trance state.

"Listen to me, Quasar. You've just eaten a spoonful of vitamin C powder. I've just given you—"

Her mouth began to work, sucking and puckering, saliva running out of the corners. That was very satisfactory; it showed good trance visualization. He tried a more advanced suggestion.

"Your arm is a steel girder standing straight up from the floor. A steel girder standing straight up out of the floor, Quasar, hard and straight and cold."

Her arm immediately rose into the air. He stood up to try and bend it—and started back in surprise.

It felt cold and hard—as steel.

He stepped close, trembling a little. The arm could bear his full weight without so much as a wobble. It was solid as the rock wall he had been sitting against. He knocked on the arm with his knuckles.

It rang like metal.

He looked in astonishment at Quasar's face. It was distant, indifferent.

"Now relax—relax your arm," he said with a tremor he hoped wouldn't break her trance. The arm slowly lowered onto the covers.

"Your—your body is getting light," he said shakily. "It's getting light as a cloud, light as a helium balloon. Your body is getting lighter and lighter; so light that it's beginning to lift up, lift off the bed and beginning to float up to the ceiling—"

When her body started to lift up, to actually lift into the air under the tattered covers, he lost his nerve.

"Come down! You're—you're getting heavy again. Heavy, very heavy. You're settling back down onto the mattress. That's it. You're settling down."

He sat dizzily against the wall. Quasar lay like a statue. It couldn't be, any more than all the other things that had happened to him could be. Her infantile personality was obviously susceptible, and his languid, detached induction had been unusually powerful, but there was no hypnotic trance that deep. Probably he had hypnotized himself as well without knowing it, and was hallucinating his own suggestions. He needed to take a few minutes to bring himself out of it—

But there wasn't *time*.

"Quasar," he quavered. "Quasar, what do you remember about—about your parents?"

"Nothing," came her voice, quiet and flat, as if from a speaker.

"What do you remember about yourself, your life?"

"Nothing."

"Quasar, listen to me. Listen to my voice. You are standing in a hallway, a big hallway that goes on a long, long way. At the end where you are the walls are almost bare, but you are going to start walking down the hallway, and you are going to look at the walls, and on the walls you will see pictures, and the pictures will be memories of all the things that have happened to you in your life, and all the things you have learned, and all the things that are inside you, even if you don't remember them. Do you see the hallway now?"

Pause. "Yes."

"I'm going to tell you to start walking down the hallway, and as you look at the pictures you will remember the things painted on them. As you go you will remember more and more, until, when you come to the end of the hallway, you will remember everything, and you will be able to hold all those memories together so that none of them are hidden. Do you understand?"

"Yes."

"All right. Start walking. Look at the pictures on the walls and remember. Concentrate on the pictures, but you will always be able to hear my voice and follow my instructions. When I ask you to describe what you are remembering, what you are seeing, do that. Start walking down the hallway."

He watched her face. It stayed calm and cold for a while, but then there was a little tic, and then another. Expressions started to flicker across it, of vague, distant happiness, anger, sadness, a haunted, worried look, then laughter.

"What do you see?" he asked.

"Mama is tickling me," lisped a very young child.

"Keep walking."

In a minute there was a cry.

"What do you see?"

There was only keening and then quiet sobbing. The CNS-HED, he guessed, when her mother had begun to "treat" her.

He sat next to her, trying to trace the expressions on her face to things he knew about her life and wondering what was going on outside the cube, how many of the mutants had gotten into the high-iso area, how soon the bombs would go off.

Quasar's face went dead grey, corpselike.

"What do you see?" Fear seized him. If by some miracle his jury-rigged hypnotherapy was causing a reintegration of her personalities, there was no telling what might happen. It was considered unsafe to attempt MPD reintegration over any time frame shorter than a year or two; how that applied to Quasar he had no idea.

"They're dead," she whispered. "They're dead. I have to follow them."

"Keep walking."

"I have to die. I can't—"

"Keep walking, Quasar."

There was a faint thump then, as if someone had dropped a heavy package on the floor outside the room.

Karmade's heart thundered. An explosion outside the cube, big enough or close enough to be heard inside.

"Quasar," he hissed. "Quasar, run. Run down the hall as fast as you can. Run as fast as you can and remember. Look at the pictures and remember. Run. Run!"

She stirred uneasily and a frown of concentration came over her face. In a minute sweat beaded on her and she began to gasp, expressions flitting over her face much faster than before.

Watching her, Karmade began to feel peculiar, vague affects running through him like currents through a wire. It was as though he somehow partook of the emotions that flickered through her so quickly, as if her nervous system was somehow broadcasting them to him—

There was another dull thump from outside.

"Run!" he hissed.

# 14

The lights were out. Karmade didn't remember them going out. He felt confused. The mutant's cube key in his hand illuminated very faintly a patch of smooth floor and nothing else. The air was dead still and neutral, the darkness completely silent. His breathing sounded painfully loud.

"Quasar?" he said. No answer. "Quasar? What happened?"

No answer.

He groped forward to touch her, orient himself. Her mattress seemed farther away than he remembered it, and then he realized he had crawled three meters and still hadn't touched it, and the entire room Quasar was in wasn't three meters across.

Panic made the hair prickle on his head. He stood up and backed toward the wall behind him.

There was no wall.

He froze, skin crawling. He forced himself to think. He had somehow gotten outside Quasar's room, into the dark place where the mutant and he had first entered the concrete cube. He couldn't remember how he had gotten here, maybe because of the cognitive distortions he had experienced watching Quasar's hypnotic trance. He had probably let himself out of the mirror door without knowing it.

It couldn't be far away. He peered into the darkness for the sheen of a mirror. He walked forward cautiously, counting his steps. At fifty he was expecting to bump into the wall of the cube. At a hundred he stopped to get his bearings. The cube was at most ten meters across. He wondered if some internal geometry made you walk in circles while you thought you were going straight ahead. He turned to the right, walked another fifty steps. He was confused now. Was his starting point behind him or to the right, and how far away?

A barely seen movement in the dark made him jump. He thought a faint stir of air touched his skin.

"Hello?" he said weakly. "Is anybody there?"

"Yes," said a voice very near him.

He jumped and spun around.

Nothing but blackness.

"Quasar?"

"Yes." Her voice was blank, indifferent.

"Where are you?"

Dead silence except for his breathing.

"Quasar?"

"Yes."

"Where are you?" Pause. "Are you there?"

He began to move in the darkness in widening circles, holding the glowing key crystal in front of him to light anything it might come near.

Nothing.

"Quasar?"

There was no answer now.

He was afraid. He caught a movement off to one side, far away through a darkness that suddenly seemed enormous.

He went toward it: a flickering smudge of light that slowly grew bigger.

And took on the shape of a softly glowing man.

It was himself, in a mirror. A gaunt man in a filthy, tattered jumpsuit, a faint light in his hand throwing shadows over his face. It was strange to see him in that place, cheeks sunken, eyes desperate and grave.

He lifted the key cube to open the mirror door.

"That mutant is a fool," said Quasar's voice, very near.

He spun around. The darkness was flat and featureless in every direction.

" 'They who sit and watch the Earth,' " she sneered, and laughed shortly. "As if They had nothing better to do than watch the viciousness and stupidity of beings ten billion years less evolved than Them."

"Quasar? Where are you?"

He listened for a while longer, but when no more words came, turned and raised the glowing cube again.

" 'Their desire to help mankind,' " Quasar mockingly mimicked the mutant. "Their desire to fuck mankind, he should have said."

"You—you know about them? Why don't you show yourself?"

"I've always known. They want to *mate* with humans. Why do you think They raped my parents when They found them where They swim in Their ocean of light? Sent them back to Earth twisted half-breed creatures? They are too perfect, incorruptible, *unchangeable;* They swim among the spheres in the unending darkness, which to Them is unending light, with no way to change, grow, *evolve.* They are too perfect; They have no way to move along the wheel of evolution except by mixing Their seed with a lower race—humans, who are change, corruption, evolution incarnate.

"This planet is enmired in suffering. Its inhabitants are in a constant state of writhing, clawing lust for what they desire, fear of what they hate. These tropisms cause dynamism, movement, change. The psychic ripples of it penetrate even the realms where They live who are perfect, unchanging, unmoving, undesiring, and thus who lack suffering, lust, fear, desire, tropism, change, evolution, *life*. And these are the things They want."

Karmade swallowed. "I am trying to—to—"

"I know what you are trying to do. And I am telling you not to waste your time.

"Do you suppose They would do anything to diminish the suffering on this planet? It is what They desire, the one thing that brings life to Their changelessness, Their perfection. Do you not think that as soon as you wake Them They will bring even greater suffering, like farmers watering their crops? Why do you think They chose the site of Their house here, in this living graveyard, the place of greatest torment on this tormented planet? Do you think for a moment They didn't lie to that mutant clown to raise the hopes of these thousands of sufferers only to dash them again?" She gave another short, cold laugh. "Go ahead, find Them and wake Them if you don't believe me, and you will see if I am not right."

"But," Karmade said weakly, "they'll have to do something or they'll die along with us. The City is going to destroy the Warrens, and this building along with everything else."

"Then you are right, we must do something. We must contact the City and tell them we are here, tell them to spare us when they destroy the mutants. There is communications hardware in this place."

"They won't listen. Your aunt—do you remember her?"

There was silence. "Vaguely," said the voice after a while, disinterestedly.

"She's behind all this. She doesn't care about the mutants—she wants to kill you and your parents. If she finds out you're here she'll make sure this place is destroyed."

"Not when she hears our offer. There is technology in this place that can make her immortal—not just cosmetically young, but really deathless. We must tell her that."

"You'd give her that?" he asked slowly. "Knowing she's insane, a murderer?"

"Your problem is that you see this issue upside down. You see that what you think of as evil is victorious on this world, triumphing over what you think of as good, and that makes you want to fight against it. You have it backward. If you want to triumph, align yourself with the triumphant. If you want to survive, align yourself with what survives. Your Nelda Cloud—my 'aunt'—is right about one thing: it is better to live forever than to die. And you will not live forever, or even a short time, if you fight the dominant force on your world.

"Now you must hurry. Turn around and walk back in the direction you came. I will guide you."

But it had come to him suddenly that Quasar or whoever was using her voice didn't want him to go through the mirror door, for reasons she wouldn't reveal was using this talk to distract him, delay him. He raised the glowing cube and made the loop-over-cross motion—

Out of the darkness a screaming figure flew, black hair flying, chalk-white features bloated, eyeholes and screaming mouth empty and hollow, bloated arms beating at him with the lightness of noisome balloons.

The mirror turned inside out and he was standing on the other side.

The terrible figure, the sloughed, somehow animated skin of Quasar Zant was gone, and in its place complete silence and stillness.

But he was not in the room with the mattress; or if he was, it had grown to enormous size. The floor was made of the same grey stone, but stretched out in vast perspective. The mirror he had come through hung on the wall just behind him, a rectangle of perfect reflection in the grey light.

Directly ahead, on a distant wall, he thought he caught the glint of another mirror.

He hesitated, then started toward it, fighting fear

and disorientation. If he kept on straight ahead maybe he would get somewhere inside this gigantic cube. And the animated skin thing had wanted to keep him from going this way, it seemed; at least from going through the mirror.

He shivered at the thought of the skin thing, wondering whether it and the enormous spaces in this place were hallucinations, whether he was hallucinating now. And if he wasn't, what did it mean? And how much time had gone by? How much time was left before they detonated the nukes, destroying this place and everything in it?

He hurried toward the mirror glint in the grey wall ahead. It was even farther away than it looked, but finally he seemed to be coming closer. And then he saw something between him and the mirror, something that gave off a hot golden glow.

He went forward warily, fearfully, but too fascinated to run away.

It was Quasar. He recognized her though she was now utterly changed. She was hairless and covered with golden scales, her hands and feet long and bone-thin with clawed fingers and toes, bony crests jutting from the top of her head. Her bright golden eyes were sharply slanted and her other features were sharp and sleek, as if streamlined for high speed.

She was beautiful. She had been beautiful as a human but not like this, with this eerie, metallic, stabbing beauty that was also terrible because he could tell that she was *hot;* heat waves rippled around her in the air like the ripples from a blast furnace; he could feel the intense radiation of it on his skin five meters away. She was lying on her side, head propped on one hand, the stone floor blackened under and around her.

His chest was tight, as if he was going to cry. He couldn't stop staring at her. He couldn't think.

She smiled and shifted position, scales glistening smoothly over powerful-looking muscles. Her teeth

were long and pointed, and her exhaled breath distorted
the air with its heat.

But her voice was rich and sweet as a golden bell.
"So you came through after all. I'm sorry if my old skin
frightened you. Going through this change I had to
shed it along with the dross of my old personality. But
all's well that ends well, isn't it?" She gave a little golden
laugh that hit him like a sledgehammer in his stomach, a
white-hot flame licking out of her mouth.

"Sit with me," she said. "No, don't come any closer;
you'll be burned. As it is you'll probably get a sunburn.
But perhaps it will be worth it." She smiled blindingly.

He sat down automatically. "Are you—are you an
exocreature? Like the—your parents?"

"Not even close. I'm heating for the next transition,
though for now I'm sane enough to talk. Have you
come to talk to me? What shall we talk about?"

He looked into her golden eyes and he couldn't
think. He didn't want to think. He wanted to sit and
look at her.

And he probably would have sat and looked at her
until the end if something had not happened.

There was a thump, as if someone had dropped a
heavy package on the floor.

"What's that?" he asked dully. "The nukes? Are they
bombing already?"

"If they are, the mutants are already dead."

He shook his head. "The high-isolation areas were
made to resist nuke attacks for a while. *Maybe there's still
time.* I've been sent to—to ask you to wake your parents."

"Then you've come on a futile mission. *I don't know
how to wake Them;* I don't even know where They are. I
haven't evolved close enough to Them yet. It will take
me a long time to get that close; years, perhaps."

He stood up sluggishly. "Then I have to try to find
them myself."

"Don't come any closer."

He tried. He could see the mirror in the wall three

meters behind her. But the heat was unbearable, so intense he had to retreat, sweat steaming from his skin. "I have to get to that—can you move?" he gasped. Then he lost his footing, stumbled forward.

She leapt up and backward with such grace and speed that she hardly seemed to move at all. He fell two meters from where she had been. His hands sizzled on the scalding floor and he scrambled back, just managing to juggle the cube key back with him. He sat a few meters away nursing his palms.

"Don't you understand?" said her beautiful voice. "What you are trying to do is impossible, futile. Even if I knew how to find Them and how to wake Them, and even if I could persuade Them to stop the bombing and rescue the mutants, what would it accomplish?

"When They do wake, They will not stay here long. Even at my stage I know that. This world is too bleak even for those who would save it. They will leave soon after They wake. And if They did save the mutants, what of it? Wouldn't the others, the ones who consider themselves normal, just slaughter them afterward? Or even if that didn't happen, do you believe it would mean the end of evil on your planet? Or would the evil just burst out again in some different place, in some different form?

"There will *always* be evil and suffering on this world. You cannot eliminate it, or even diminish it one iota, by saving the mutants; nothing but a fundamental restructuring of the laws of nature could do that. And that is not something They can accomplish. So by doing what you wish you would be achieving nothing."

"But—"

"Sit and talk to me," said the Quasar-creature. "Distract me for a while from my pain. Watch me change if you wish—if you can bear it—"

But as she lay down again, stretching out lithely on the floor, he scrambled up and dashed past her.

He had surprised her in an awkward position. He was nearly to the mirror before she caught him, her breath scorching his back like a blowtorch, his arm and shoulder exploding in unbearable pain where she grabbed him. In the mirror he glimpsed a figure engulfed in flame and greasy smoke, face a death mask of agony, one clawed, outstretched hand moving a crystal cube—

The mirror reached out and sucked him through.

This was a place of illusion, he knew as he stood shivering in freezing, blinding light on the other side of the mirror. There was not a burn anywhere on him now, nor any pain except that of cold. He was standing in an enormous place like the previous one, but here the walls and floor and even the air glowed white, as if made of some intense, pure form of lumtile, and it was cold.

It came to him that someone or something was trying to stop him from doing what the black-robed mutant—who seemed unreal and distant now—had told him to do. He wondered vaguely who and why, trying at the same time to remind himself exactly what the mutant had wanted.

If this place was like the last two there was a mirror doorway straight ahead, though he couldn't see it in the brightness. Karmade started jogging, then running in that direction, wrapping his arms around himself against the cold.

The place was very big. Karmade ran on and on until he heard music.

It was faint and celestial, coming from the air around him, and when it came the white light seemed to eddy like snow, forming a shape briefly, as if the music had imposed a waveform on it. When it trailed off into silence the eddy whirled itself away in the freezing light.

Karmade ran on, hoping he was going straight ahead but unable to tell exactly.

Music sighed again and a shape emerged toward him out of the air, the outline of a female figure—but no; as he got closer it too was just a trick of the light—

But when it came the third time, and he stumbled and fell trying not to hit it, the form hardened and froze, the music wisping light around it like a cloak, a glow brightening inside it with a hum to blinding intensity, and it was *alive;* it moved its hands and looked at him from crystal eyes—

It was Quasar again, but this time transparent, crystalline, filled with light. The light waxed and waned, and when it waxed it filled the air with an intense hum that vibrated Karmade's body as if to disintegrate it.

In the vibration was a radiation of *feeling,* an intense restfulness and bliss, so that he knelt on the freezing floor basking in warmth and comfort even as his physical body shook with cold. Then he put his head down and curled up at her feet.

She didn't speak, but meanings radiated in the celestial music that was the waveform of her body.

That's right, rest, she seemed to say. Rest. Where are you going in such a hurry? Does the River of Souls not move fast enough for you? Patience. Is there anywhere you can hurry to? You are already there, can you not see?

He could see.

"But the mutants." He lifted his head and sobbed when he heard the faint thumps from outside, now many of them. "They'll all die, and I have to—and we'll die—"

You are in the River of Souls, said the serene music. And so are they. And so are all of us. Do you think we could ever be lost? Be somehow misplaced in the cosmic design? It laughed sweetly. You are eternal, do you not know? Dying is like waking from a dream. Being born is like waking again. We go on and on, sleeping and waking, higher and higher, seeing ever more and more of the Pattern, and the more we see, the less reason there is to struggle, to run, to fight. Do you understand?

He understood.

Her hands, crystalline but soft as feathers, caressed him as he lay, her breath, cold but scented like rose petals, touched his face. The hum from the glowing center of her warmed and soothed him even as he heard and felt the thumps intensify outside the cube, even as he knew he was freezing to death.

Another waking from a dream . . .

Even so, he dragged himself to the mirror glinting in the white light a little way off, and moved the crystal key loop over cross—

He woke in the twisted ruins of the cube, on a floor that felt like stone but was buckled like metal, a split-open wall letting dim outside light fall across a ruin of alien-looking machinery and circuitry. The cube looked no more than ten meters across now that it was wrecked, and Karmade wondered dully how they had managed the previous illusion of size.

But that question was now academic, he realized as a wisp of smoke drifted in through the split wall.

A distant thundering came from outside the cube, like giant engines straining to do some mighty work. Karmade stumbled to his feet and climbed up the tilted floor to the rift in the wall.

Outside, the Warrens were a nightmare jumble of destruction: concrete rubble and twisted metal heaped in kipple mountains and scooped away in craters, lit strangely from below so that vast shadows rose above it all. The illumination came from a crater yawning below the mountain of rubble where the cube lay; at the bottom of it arc lights had been set up over huge tanks and gigantic pipes snaking into a jagged, dark hole in the ground.

Biocides. The tiny figures of androids tended the giant pumps driving millions of liters of biocides into the high-isolation shelter where the mutants had gone to hide, every blind and dog-limbed and telepathic one of them, with their old-faced babies who had never known anything but hunger, and the wrinkled, black-robed man who had wanted to save them—all dead now, erased from the world.

And as the androids worked their way up the crater and pumped the rest of the smoking chasm that had been the underground city full of their poison, Karmade knew that he would die too, and the Zant exocreatures if they weren't already dead, if they had ever existed at all.

Or if the androids moved slowly the radioactivity from the nuke blasts might get them first, he guessed.

Either way, Nelda Cloud had won.

The thought filled him with rage. He remembered her laughing face, her light, exciting voice talking as if about a particularly lovely party as her androids wiped the blood off her beautiful body. She was a creature without feelings, the humanness drained out of her malfunctioning nervous system so that she was just a cybernetic mechanism like the androids in the crater below. Yet she had defeated the living: the mutants and her desperate, crazy niece.

A moan came from the air beside him. He whirled in panic, but nothing was there. Perhaps it had been the groan of some metal part of the cube sagging, or maybe he was hallucinating. But it didn't matter. Nothing mattered now.

Except—

He scrambled shakily out through the split wall and onto the rubble where the cube lay upended. A meter's length of melted-off reinforcing steel stuck out between chunks of shattered concrete. He picked it up and made his way slowly down the slope of destruction.

He tried to go quietly. He was creeping between two huge concrete slabs when he heard the sound of someone walking. He froze against one of the slabs.

A patrolling android, its crude rubber head rotating on its neck, walked by, an autocannon snapped into one of its arm sockets.

Karmade jumped out and swung his metal bar with the strength of rage.

The android's head snapped off and tumbled among the rocks. Its body, frozen in midstride, fell over stiffly, shaking and rattling in the rubble.

Another moan sounded in the air and sweaty hands seemed to grab Karmade's wrists.

He whirled around, and around again. No one was there. Nothing was touching him. The only sound was the distant scream of the biocide pumps.

Karmade exchanged his metal bar for the android's autocannon.

He crept farther down the wall of the crater. Soon the enormous white spheres of the biocide tanks loomed over the rubble he crouched behind. His breath hissed between his teeth.

He passed two androids with their backs to him, and a third figure—a bulbous, vehiclelike suit of combat armor that contained one of the androids' human handlers —twisting the controls on a room-sized pump. The bitter tang of biocide stung the air; as Karmade breathed it his eyes went dark, his heart labored.

Just a few more steps.

The huge moon of a biocide tank bulked above him. He could see the ribs in its plastic sides, hear its bloated humming as he leaned against a warm hump of rock, lifted his autocannon.

He screamed in rage, exhilaration, and defeat as the fiery slashes from the cannon's rounds tore and widened with the pressure of the tank's contents, until it burst like an enormous, noisome boil, hyper-poisonous white liquid descending in slow motion with an earth-shaking roar, washing the pumps and the android soldiers and Karmade into the black, smoking tomb-hole at the bottom of the crater.

In his ears a rising, convulsive panting became a scream.

# 15

Another awakening—

Delicate, glazed black eyes fluttered open and blood-gorged lips parted to take a hissing breath. Karmade's palms pressed against heaving, muscular shoulders, and strong hands held his wrists.

"Unh," the breath moaned out of Quasar's mouth, hot and aromatic on his face.

He was up, standing over her in panic.

Her naked body was still arching, rocking on the mattress.

"It's happening," she hissed, closing her eyes again. "You and your goddamn *hallway of memories*—"

She held her hands out to him, sweat running down her arms.

"Where—where am I?" Disorientation made him feel cold, nauseous.

She laughed raucously. "You didn't like that? That was *It thinking*—except with It, everyone feels and sees what It thinks." She was shivering convulsively, with cold or excitement or fear he couldn't tell.

His teeth started to chatter. He stared around the room, grasping the fact that it was still undamaged, that the cube's destruction and what had gone before had been hallucinations.

Quasar laughed, and he could see the pain in her face. She got up on her elbow with difficulty. "Don't you understand? You woke It when you brought back my memories. Its mind is so strong It broadcasts to everything around It. Just now It was—testing you, I think—testing your resolve, or your worthiness to rescue It, or the resolve of the human race to rescue itself, or something like that. I don't understand exactly—It doesn't think like we do. It's resting now, but only for a little while. It will come again, and this time—" She trembled wildly, her body jerking uncontrollably. "The sooner the better. It hurts to be halfway—"

Her voice broke and she jerked backward onto the mattress, arms and legs straining as her body arched, muscles and tendons standing out like cords. As she shrieked Karmade saw with horror that her lower abdomen was swelling and gnarling upward, as if something —something strong—was fighting to get out.

The swelling subsided and she lay gasping. Trickles of blood came from her mouth and vagina. She opened her eyes again and smiled peacefully.

"You see?" she whispered. "I don't want to be me anymore. It hurts too much. Listen: when—it happens, it will look like I've died, or am dying. But I'm not me anymore, you understand? I'm—something else. So it won't matter. Please don't cry."

She sat up painfully and took his hand, pulled him down to her as he sobbed, overwhelmed, his reason overthrown.

For a minute he floated in her arms, rocked on the waves of her breath, feeling the motion of the planet as it soared in the dark.

Then she was screaming and her stomach was splitting open.

"D-d-down. D-d-down," she chattered, then shrieked again, her blood spattering him.

A square of stone blocks in one of the walls dissolved into nothingness, the dark opening showing descending stairs.

Quasar jerked and thrashed grotesquely now without consciousness, as if her body was controlled by something nonhuman that gurgled horribly in her throat.

Karmade picked her up and started down the stairs in panic, cursing and praying.

He went far down, and as he went it got colder until at the bottom his breath was solid gouts of fog. Quasar now hung unconscious in his arms, a hideous split in her stomach leaking dark blood that steamed in the cold. Karmade's skin burned with cold.

A stone passage, colder even than the stairs, was lit by a glow that seemed to follow them, leaving the parts a meter ahead and behind in darkness. Karmade's boots scuffled drunkenly on the stone. He was almost unconscious with cold, his body numb, eyelids frozen almost shut, a beard of frost forming around his lips and nostrils. At the end of the passage was a blank wall.

Maybe there were sensors in the wall that read Quasar's brain field. He couldn't tell. There was a massive cracking, then a rumbling and screeching, and air blew past violently from the tunnel behind him as the wall split in two and swung inward. The wind stopped and motes of ice it had swept up twinkled in the air of the place inside, which Karmade guessed had been held in vacuum until now.

And in there—

The chamber was ten meters on a side, floor, walls, and ceiling made of the same stone blocks as the passage. Filling half of it were two *things,* two enormous, hideous cocoons clinging to the inner wall and almost reaching the ten-meter ceiling, gnarled and knotted and shriveled as if whatever had grown inside them was done with its cocoon stage.

The place was deadly cold, cold as interplanetary

space; Karmade could feel it draining away his remaining consciousness.

Quasar stirred in his arms.

"Leave me," she whispered.

"Too cold," his frozen lips mumbled.

She shook her head and smiled a little. "You don't understand? Still don't understand?" She closed her eyes, resting from the effort of talking. For a minute he thought she had lost consciousness again, but then her eyes fluttered open. "Please," she said, almost too faint to hear. "Please." A twinge of pain made her stiffen in his arms.

He knelt and put her on the searing-cold floor, terrified suddenly of seeing her hurt more. She smiled sweetly, peacefully. She didn't seem able to talk. Her flesh was freezing solid.

He turned and ran, ran from her death, from the horrible shapes towering above her, up the stairs to the little room with the mattress, and in the instant before the stone wall solidified behind him a rattling shriek echoed distantly, a cry of inconceivable pain.

The wall cut it off.

He had lost the key cube somewhere. There was no way out of the room. He lay on the mattress and thought feverishly, looking up at the stone ceiling, thought back over the last days, trying to figure out if he had done well or ill. Had he been the cause of Tom Rothe's death at Nelda Cloud's hands? Of the deaths of the sewer tribesmen who had taken him through the Boundary Zone, of the mutants in the tunnel above the Boundary Zone? Would it have been better if they had lived and he had died or been captured? Had it been necessary to kill the mutant in Death Hole Warren? And all the mutants who were going to die unless Quasar woke the exocreatures—had he done all he could to save them? Had he hurried? Had he fought hard enough? Could he have headed off all this disaster by resisting the temptation to go to Quasar at Hak Lun's Dusk House, in a time that now seemed dreamlike and far away—?

All these things seemed important; more important by far than whether he would die in this room. He felt like a soul lying in the grave on the eve of Judgment Day, counting up its sins and merits, trying to guess its fate.

After a while something stirred below him.

It was a vibration, almost a deep, powerful sound, as if a voice too deep to hear had spoken beneath the earth. The vibration intensified to a shaking that sent the sanitary module rattling across the floor and Karmade leaping off the mattress in animal terror. In a minute a full-blown earthquake rippled the walls of the room, the close-set stone blocks grinding and cracking. Dust and stone chips showered down. Karmade briefly wondered if it was the cocoon shapes downstairs moving or the nuke blasts starting, and then something else came brimming up through the rock to him.

A *feeling*.

It had crept up slowly, he realized, after he had left Quasar in the freezing chamber, had grown gradually as he lay in this room, feeding his wonderings and calculations: a strange, intense clarity of the kind he had felt making love to Quasar, and for a moment treating her on the CNS-HED. But stronger now and steadier, and somehow *natural*, as though its absence, which he had lived with all his life, had been a kind of trance or mental defect. It was as though a fog had cleared away, letting him see things clearly for the first time. He had a fleeting image of himself standing in a high place, looking down through a vast, clear atmosphere at a land of snow-capped mountains, green plains, and rivers, a world whose true pattern he was seeing for the first time—

It flashed on him that he was experiencing brain functioning optimization, something people had been trying to produce with drugs, therapy, and machines—and before that herbs, meditation, and religion—for thousands of years. Somehow his brain had been entrained into an extremely high-functioning state, the transition taking place over just a few minutes. It al-

lowed him to think steadily and quickly even as the
building began to come apart around him.

He could see that if the room collapsed slowly rather
than all at once he should try to climb up and out of it
so as to be on top of as much of the rubble as possible.
Of course, it was more likely he would be crushed. He
picked up Quasar's mattress and held it over him as a
kind of shield, trying to stay upright against the angry
shaking of the floor.

—and that taken care of, cast his thoughts out across
their vast new landscape in what might be the last few
seconds available to him, and grasped finally the structure of his life and the life of his race, seeing with sudden
devastating clarity what he had seen only in glimpses
before, that the human species had become insane, the
result of an insane past and the psychological distortions
devised to rationalize it. He understood abruptly the
City's projection of the evils it had invented upon the
mutants, that the Mayor and City Council were soci-
opathic paranoids controlled by the same industrial/cy-
bernetic complex that had sold the human race into its
wars, and which ran the City, and which had no human
agenda because it was not human but an intricate system
of machines the human race had entrusted with its safe-
keeping—

Two stone blocks cracked out of the undulating wall
and fell half on top of his mattress, letting him wriggle
out from under them and squeeze through the hole they
had left, scrambling and clawing. Stone split above him,
tumbled around and under him, giving him the dizzying
feeling of climbing a narrow tunnel that was falling away
beneath his feet.

Then with a roar the building collapsed, tons of
stone and metal thundering down—

—and something lifted him. Something hard and big
lifted him quick and smooth as an express transvator. He
could hear the building falling around and above him,
metal shrieking, stone grinding, but nothing hit him. He
couldn't open his eyes because of the showering dust—

Until he was set down on something that trembled but didn't fall, and then through billowing dust he could see grey light and vast space and movement—

He blinked his eyes clear, smudged them with a dirt-caked forearm, coughed dust out of his lungs. And abruptly sat down.

He was on a blasted column of concrete jutting twenty meters above the shattered cube structure. He wondered if he was hallucinating again, lying crushed under tons of rock. There had been intensive bombing in the underground city, he saw, though maybe not yet with nukes: concrete and metal and stone were heaved up into still-smoking heaps and hills just as in his earlier hallucination, his column jutting out of one of them so that he looked down into a deep crater that laid bare the blast-scoured but still unbroken shell of the high-isolation shelter where the mutants hid.

And down the slope of the crater and across the wide landscape of smoking destruction a vast, silent army moved in perfect lock-step formation, an army of City androids heading toward the bared high-iso shell, missile launchers rolling silently among them on caterpillar tracks like docile insects.

Suddenly up into the air between the destruction and the high-arching, pocked concrete roof of the blast-hollowed underground city rose three *things*.

They were flying away from Karmade, obscured by dim light and billowing smoke, yet somehow he saw them clearly. He guessed the image was telepathic, an impression made directly on the brain regardless of their distance or orientation. Certainly they were the source of the clarity and steadiness that filled him; it radiated unmistakably from them like heat or light, a kind of mental light that cut through the shadows of fear, delusion, and anger that had clogged him for so long.

As he saw them, distant yet magnified in his consciousness, they were black Eyes, flying on fans of energy whose visible penumbra vaguely resembled wings, hideous and gorgeous, terrifying and stately and grave;

three Eyes, one smaller—less vivid, less powerful—than the two others. Yet at the same time he knew they were not really Eyes, that the Eye images were symbols by which they represented themselves to humans, *things* that could not otherwise be grasped or made sense of.

As the three of them rose into the air he saw that it was not only living eyes they mesmerized, for all at once the whole silent army of androids stopped marching. Then they all turned in a single motion to watch the Eyes, raising their ten thousand incurious machine faces in endless files of ignorant, involuntary worship.

They froze like that, they and their missiles, and they never moved again. They were left down there in the pitch-dark that descended after their lights were taken away, as a memorial and a warning.

The Eyes on their wings of energy rose quickly to the concrete roof of the underground city and out the jagged hole the City had blasted for the passage of its army.

Inside the high-isolation shelter the mutants must have felt something—the same thing Karmade felt sitting breathless on the column of blasted concrete—for a few minutes later there was a metal screeching and the automated hatch on the high-iso shell jerkily and with a rasping of hundred-year-old threads slowly unscrewed itself, and a dozen pale, ragged shapes gawked out.

Karmade never saw the Eyes again.

But it was reported that three huge *things* hovered over the City that night for an hour. The TV news reports gave them a hundred different shapes and qualities, but every human in the City knew what they were.

Sudden sanity acts in different ways on different people. The Mayor and several City Councilmembers shot themselves. Nelda Cloud was found decapitated on her own torture chamber table, beautiful hands clenched on the controls. Dr. Ziller's head was later found in Cloud's collection, and mercifully euthanatized along with the rest.

Karmade struggled up to the surface with the first of the mutants, a long, ragged line of silent figures scrambling and climbing and helping each other through the holes and shafts that had been blasted down from the surface, tiptoeing fearfully past war machines and Maggots frozen by the previous ascent of the Eyes, holding hands in terror and hope as a breath of cool air blew down past them through the blackened cavity. But when they climbed up into the enormous excavation that had been dug in the 12th Sector as a staging area for the sterilization operation, a huge suit of motorized combat armor rushed them, scattering the screaming mutants, except for one tiny girl. She stood frozen with fear, dropping her ragged doll in the mud at the armor's feet.

Her mother's shrieks came from behind boulders where the cowering mutants held her.

The armor slowly and with a humming of motors knelt in the mud and picked up the doll in one of its enormous claws. It picked up the little girl carefully with the other.

Then the headpiece hummed open, and the pale face of the human man inside looked into the face of the human child.

# ABOUT THE AUTHOR

JAMIL NASIR was born in Chicago, Illinois of a Palestinian refugee father and the American daughter of the inventor of the fork-lift truck. He spent much of his childhood in the Middle East, where he survived two major wars, hiding in cellars and storerooms with his family. He returned to the United States and started college at age 14, studying hard sciences, philosophy of science, English literature, psychology, and Chinese literature and philosophy, finally graduating from the University of Michigan in Ann Arbor with a Bachelors of General Studies.

Between college stints he hitchhiked extensively over much of North America, working as a carpenter, assistant gardener on an estate, shop clerk, warehouseman, apple-picker, and paralegal, among others. He finally found himself back in Ann Arbor, where he got a law degree in 1983. Since then he has been employed part-time at a major Washington, D.C. law firm.

He has sold science fiction stories to *Asimov's*, *Universe* (vols. 1, 2, and 3), *Interzone*, *Aboriginal SF*, and a number of other magazines and anthologies, including Steve Pasechnick's 1990 best-of-the-year anthology *Best of the Rest,* and Dozois' and Dann's *Angels!,* a reprint anthology. He won a First Prize in the 1988 Writers of the Future competition.

Mr. Nasir meditates three hours a day, likes to cook, listen to music, play computer games, read, and walk. He lives with his wife and two small daughters in the Maryland countryside 25 miles outside Washington. QUASAR is his first novel.

# A SPECIAL PREVIEW

*From the pens of three of science fiction's brightest stars
come three long-awaited sequels. Any one alone would
be an event of note. All three together
is nothing short of a Grand Event.*

## BRIGHTNESS REEF
## BY DAVID BRIN

DAVID BRIN'S Uplift novels form one of the most thrilling science
fiction sagas ever written, set in a world brimming with imagina-
tion. The *New York Times* bestselling series has received two Hugo
Awards and a Nebula Award. Now, after an eight-year absence,
David Brin finally returns to his most popular universe with the first
book in an all-new Uplift trilogy. *on sale now*

## BLADE RUNNER™ 2: THE EDGE OF HUMAN
## BY K. W. JETER

FANS EVERYWHERE are familiar with director Ridley Scott's dark,
stylish, futuristic masterpiece. Now, K. W. Jeter—popularly known
as the heir to Philip K. Dick—returns to the steamy streets of
twenty-first-century Los Angeles with the continuing adventure of
Rick Deckard, a Blade Runner charged with the execution of rene-
gade replicants. *on sale now*

## ENDYMION
## BY DAN SIMMONS

DAN SIMMONS'S brilliant novels *Hyperion* and *The Fall of Hyperion*
are among the most thunderously applauded science fiction publi-
cations of the last decade, and new readers constantly delight in
discovering the awe and wonder of Simmons's gloriously realized
far-future universe. Now he returns to continue the immortal tale
of mankind's destiny among the stars. *Coming in December 1995.*

*Help us celebrate our Tenth Anniversary with
these blockbuster Spectra hardcovers!*

TM: © The Blade Runner Partnership 1982

SF 13 11/95

# BANTAM SPECTRA

CELEBRATES ITS TENTH ANNIVERSARY IN 1995!

With more HUGO and NEBULA AWARD winners
than any other science fiction and fantasy publisher

With more classic and cutting-edge fiction
coming every month

Bantam Spectra is proud to be the leading
publisher of fantasy and science fiction

---

KEVIN J. ANDERSON • ISAAC ASIMOV • IAIN M. BANKS •
GREGORY BENFORD • BEN BOVA • RAY BRADBURY •
MARION ZIMMER BRADLEY • DAVID BRIN • ARTHUR C.
CLARKE • THOMAS DEHAVEN • STEPHEN R. DONALDSON
• RAYMOND E. FEIST • JOHN M. FORD • MAGGIE FUREY •
DAVID GERROLD • WILLIAM GIBSON • STEPHAN GRUNDY •
ELIZABETH HAND • HARRY HARRISON • ROBIN HOBB •
JAMES HOGAN • KATHARINE KERR • GENTRY LEE • URSULA
K. LEGUIN • VONDA N. MCINTYRE • LISA MASON • ANNE
MCCAFFREY • IAN MCDONALD • DENNIS L. MCKIERNAN
• WALTER M. MILLER, JR. • DANIEL KEYS MORAN • LINDA
NAGATA •JAMIL NASIR• KIM STANLEY ROBINSON • ROBERT
SILVERBERG • DAN SIMMONS • MICHAEL A. STACKPOLE •
NEAL STEPHENSON • BRUCE STERLING • TRICIA SULLIVAN
• SHERI S.TEPPER • PAULA VOLSKY • MARGARET WEIS AND
TRACY HICKMAN • ELISABETH VONARBURG • ANGUS
WELLS • CONNIE WILLIS • DAVE WOLVERTON • TIMOTHY
ZAHN • ROGER ZELAZNY AND ROBERT SHECKLEY

---